SUMMER PASSION

What Reviewers Say About MJ Williamz's Work

"MJ Williamz, in her first romantic thriller has done an impressive job of building up the tension and suspense. Williamz has a firm grasp of keeping the reader guessing and quickly turning the pages to get to the bottom of the mystery. *Shots Fired* clearly shows the author's ability to spin an engaging tale and is sure to be just the beginning of great things to follow as the author matures."—*Lambda Literary*

"The love story is well written and the characters are multi-dimensional. *Forbidden Passions* is the very model of modern major erotica, but hidden within the sweet swells and trembling clefts of that erotica is a beautiful May-September romance between two wonderful and memorable characters. M.J. Williamz has a wide reputation for her short stories, and has now given her fans a sound and playful second novel."—*The Rainbow Reader*

Visit us at www.boldstrokesbooks.com

By the Author

Shots Fired

Forbidden Passions

Initiation by Desire

Speakeasy

Escapades

Sheltered Love

Summer Passion

SUMMER PASSION

by

MJ Williamz

2015

ISBN 13: 978-1-62639-540-4

This Trade Paperback Original Is Published By
Bold Strokes Books, Inc.
P.O. Box 249
Valley Falls, NY 12185

First Edition: November 2015

Credits
Editor: Cindy Cresap
Production Design: Susan Ramundo
Cover Design By Sheri (graphicartist2020@hotmail.com)

Acknowledgments

First and foremost, I'd like to thank my wife, Laydin, for all her support and encouragement. I truly don't think I'd get through a book without her. Next, I'd like to thank Sarah, who is my number one reader.

Next, I'd like to thank Radclyffe for giving us a place where our stories can be heard. A special thank you goes to Cindy, my editor, who works tirelessly trying to make me a better writer.

Dedication

For Laydin—Forever

CHAPTER ONE

"Cut!" the director yelled. "That's a wrap. Good job, everyone."

Jean Sanders walked off the set and into her dressing room. She felt good about the scenes they had shot that day. She sat and lit a cigarette, inhaling deeply. While there were certain things about being America's Sweetheart in 1946 that were draining, having her private dressing room was certainly not one of them.

She was happy with the new movie they were filming. It wasn't a musical or a Western, which were so prevalent right then. It was a heart-wrenching movie about a woman struggling to overcome the loss of her husband during the war. She thought she was playing the part well.

Her thoughts were interrupted by a knock on her door.

"Come."

"Miss Sanders, Mr. Duvall has invited you to dinner," one of the stagehands said. David Duvall was the director. He was queer as a three-dollar bill, so she knew it was safe to go out with him. And they often dined together. She was glad she hadn't unrolled her hair yet.

"Tell him I'll be out in twenty minutes."

She washed off the thick makeup she wore for the cameras and skillfully applied her everyday makeup. She finished by applying deep red lipstick and stood. She slipped out of her costume and into a nice dress for dinner. She knew David wanted to show her off and would only take her to an upscale restaurant.

Jean checked herself out in the mirror and, satisfied, stepped onto the set again to find David sitting in his chair waiting for her.

"My darling Jean, you look radiant."

"Thank you, David."

"I thought we'd have Italian tonight. Barichelli's sound good to you?"

"Sounds delicious. I'm famished."

❖

It was a pleasant Hollywood evening. The air was cool but not chilly, and Jean was comfortable in her dress. They drove off the set and to the Sunset Strip, the section of Hollywood where people went to see and be seen.

David handed his keys to the valet, then helped Jean out of the car.

"You sure know how to make an exit," he said. "You've got the shapeliest legs in the business."

"Why, David, you'll make me blush."

"I don't think that's possible."

She took his arm and smiled as the cameras around them flashed and took their pictures. She was used to it. And she was used to the rumors linking her with David. It worked for both of them, so they let the gossips wag their tongues.

They managed to get inside the restaurant, where David slipped the maître d' a twenty-dollar bill to be seated soon. It worked and soon they were at a table in the center of the restaurant. If it was privacy they had wanted, they would have found a different spot. Several times during the meal, people came up and asked Jean for her autograph, which she graciously provided.

"Your public loves you," David said.

"Yes, they do. And they will love me even more once *Scars of the Heart* comes out."

"Isn't it a masterpiece of a movie? I've no doubt it'll be a smash."

"Well, tomorrow is another early day on the set," Jean said. "You should probably get me home."

"Yes, dear. I'll drop you off. And, of course, I'll send a car for you in the morning."

"Thank you."

❖

They drove to Jean's estate several miles outside of town. It was a lovely, rambling house surrounded by well-kept gardens in the middle of an orange grove.

"As always, it was a pleasure, my dear."

"Yes, it was, David. Thank you again. I'll see you tomorrow."

She got out of the car and let herself in her front door.

"I was beginning to wonder if you were ever coming home," her maid, Betty, who was sitting on a white leather chair said.

"Betty. I didn't realize you were still here."

Betty was Jean's longtime maid. She sat in her maid uniform with her legs stretched out before her, clad in fishnet stockings.

The high heels she had on clearly indicated she wasn't there to clean the house.

"I took a shower after I finished and thought I'd wait and see what kind of mood you were in when you got home."

Jean walked behind Betty and lightly dragged her fingers along one side of her neck while she nuzzled the other side.

"Mm. You smell good."

"I used your favorite powder."

"My Betty is in a mood tonight, aren't you?"

"Well, I wanted to please you, Ms. Sanders."

"And be pleased by me, perhaps?"

Jean watched the flush pass over Betty. She loved knowing Betty was so anxious for her. She always enjoyed their playtime. Betty was the only person she role-played with and they had such fun at it.

She slid her hand down the front of Betty's maid uniform and closed it on a full breast.

"Oh, Betty. You were made for pleasure. Stand up for me."

Betty did as she was told. Jean walked around her, checking her out.

"Take off that dress," she said.

Betty started to unbutton it, and Jean reached out and grabbed her hand.

"Slowly."

Betty slowed down and unbuttoned her dress, letting it slip off her shoulders and land in a heap on the floor.

Jean walked around her again, admiring her full figure. She was sexy as hell in her thigh-high stockings. She was glad she hadn't bothered with panties. They were a waste of time and Jean seldom wore them herself.

She stood in front of Betty, staring into her eyes. She loved the passion she saw burning there.

"Do you want me, Betty?"

"Oh, yes."

Jean kissed her then, a soft, light kiss.

"You taste good. You taste like wine. Did you have some of my wine?"

"Just a glass."

"Good. I don't want you to be numb. I want you alert to feel everything."

"I want that, too."

Jean put one hand behind Betty's head and pulled her to her, kissing her passionately on the mouth. Betty's mouth opened immediately, and Jean thrust her tongue inside and slipped her other hand between Betty's legs to feel how wet and ready she was for her. She plunged her fingers inside as she continued to move her tongue in her mouth.

She felt Betty moan into her mouth as she neared her climax. She continued to work her fingers until Betty collapsed against her.

"Is that what you needed?" Jean asked.

"Oh, yes."

Jean took her hand and led her to the couch. She laid her back and placed one leg over the back of the couch. She climbed between her legs and lapped up the evidence of her orgasm. She continued to lick every inch of her, spending more time on her clit, which she knew to be hypersensitive. In no time at all, Betty was calling out her name.

"May I please you now, Ms. Sanders?" Betty asked.

"Not tonight. I have an early call."

"Okay." Betty was clearly disappointed.

"I'm sorry I got home so late. Had I known you were waiting, perhaps I would have forgone dinner out. But you know I need to be seen out and about on occasion."

"I understand. I'll get dressed and see myself out. Thank you, though. I had a swell time."

"As did I."

She kissed her good night and went to her room.

She slipped out of her clothes and climbed between her silky soft sheets. The feel of the fabric on her bare skin did little to cool the heat she was feeling after fucking Betty. She reached between her legs and found her clit swollen and slick. She should have let Betty take care of her, but she had to get up early and it wouldn't do to show up on the set with dark circles under her eyes. Still, she couldn't sleep and felt that a clit that hard shouldn't be wasted.

She closed her eyes and thought about Dorothy Martin, the woman she costarred with in her last movie. Her dark eyes and sensual smile had teased Jean for months. She imagined Dorothy's long fingers caressing her as she stroked between her legs. She fantasized about playing with Dorothy's voluptuous breasts as she pleased herself. As everything she saw in her mind's eye played out, Jean brought herself to a powerful orgasm.

❖

Filming went well for the next few weeks, and soon *Scars of the Heart* was a wrap. Jean threw a tremendous party at her estate. All the stars were there, including Dorothy Martin. Jean did her best to charm the cold woman, to no avail. She was a frustrated mess as she wandered the grounds seeing women making out with each other and men doing the same. She needed to find a woman to bed.

A woman she didn't know approached her.

"Ms. Sanders? Jean Sanders? Oh, my God. I can't believe it's really you."

"Who else would it be? It's my house."

"I know. But there are so many people here. I never dreamed I'd actually meet you."

Jean was intrigued. The young woman was clearly a fan. But she was a very attractive fan. Which made it very tempting for Jean to attempt to seduce her. But she couldn't take a chance. Her sexuality had to stay out of the public's eye. She wondered how this woman had gotten into the party. She knew everyone at the party, or so she thought. She did that specifically to keep her sexuality and that of her friends private. So who was this woman?

"Well, it's a pleasure to meet you," Jean said.

"The pleasure is mine. I'm thrilled to meet you."

"Thank you. That's very nice of you to say."

"I know it's not right to ask for an autograph at a party like this..." the woman said.

"How did you hear about this party?" Jean finally asked.

"I came with Dorothy Martin."

"You did?" Jean was intrigued.

"Yes. You might say I'm her date."

"Date, date?"

"Well, I don't know how to answer that."

"Answer it honestly," Jean said. "You can tell me. What do you think I am? An old fuddy duddy?"

"I should probably go find Dorothy."

"Okay. Well, again, it was nice meeting you."

"Nice meeting you, too."

Jean watched the woman walk off and enjoyed the view.

Her curiosity and libido piqued, she wandered back to the house to see what was happening there. People were dancing in the ballroom. Others were relaxing in the sitting rooms. Everyone seemed to be having fun.

She saw Betty serving her guests and watched as several women made passes at her. She smiled. She knew Betty was probably more than they could handle. She also knew Betty knew she was working at the moment so every woman was off limits.

The sexual mood of the party did nothing to cool her needs. Hollywood was a place where lesbians had to be secretive, but at her parties, everyone was free. If only she could find someone to be free with.

Jean felt the gaze on her before she noticed the brunette watching her from across the room. She looked vaguely familiar with green eyes that called to Jean. Where did she know her from? She tried to remember before she crossed the room. She needn't have worried. The woman approached her, as well.

"Hello, Jean. It's good to see you again."

Jean panicked. So she did know the woman. But how?

"You don't remember me," the woman said. "I don't blame you. I was an extra on the set of *Nights in Miami*. You were always so nice to me. I appreciated that."

"Of course! That's how I know you. I knew you looked familiar. How goes the career?"

"I've been getting bigger and bigger parts lately. I'm hoping to be famous like you someday."

"Forgive me," Jean said, "But your name escapes me."

"Oh, I'm sorry. My name is Margaret. But you can call me Maggie."

"It's good to see you again, Maggie." Jean searched for something to say. Maggie's long brown hair and piercing green eyes had Jean hoping for more than a casual conversation with her. "Can I get you something to drink?"

"I'd love a martini."

"Done. Would you like to come with me or wait for me here?"

"I'll join you, if you don't mind."

"I don't mind at all."

They walked back to the quiet area that was Jean's bar.

"So, Maggie. Do you have a last name?"

"Cranston."

"Excellent. I hope to see Margaret Cranston in big lights some day."

"Thank you. You have been my idol for years. I hope I make it like you have."

"Well, it sounds like you're on your way. Bigger parts are always a good thing. Tell me, what kind of roles are you looking for?"

"The usual...a romantic lead. I'm not that interested in horror movies. I like good old-fashioned romances."

Jean nodded.

"Not to say I wouldn't take a role like that if it came along. But that's not where my heart lies."

"I understand. Let's take this conversation outside."

Jean took Maggie's hand and led her into her small, personal garden. No one else was allowed there, so they had plenty of privacy.

"So where did you get your training, Maggie?"

"I went to Bryn Mawr."

"That's a good school."

"I also did some stock work. I think I'm proving myself a good actress."

"You did good work on *Miami*, as I recall. I'm sure you're making a name for yourself."

"Thank you. That means the world to me."

"And what do you do in your free time? What are some of your interests?"

"I like to read and, of course, practice my acting."

"What do you like to read?"

"I like Gertrude Stein and Radclyffe Hall."

Jean understood exactly what Maggie was saying. She was safe. She, too, was a lesbian and Jean could relax and be free with her.

"I've read Hall as well. It was fairly depressing."

"Yes. But it was so nice to read about people like me. Like us?"

"Yes. Like us."

Maggie smiled. Her whole face lit up. Her eyes sparkled. Jean could see the want in them.

"Would you like another drink?" Jean asked.

"Sure."

They made their way back into the house. When Jean took Maggie's glass from her, their fingers touched and Jean felt the shock to her core. She knew she would have to have Maggie, and soon.

Drinks in hand, they meandered back to the garden.

"Can I show you around?" Jean asked.

"I'd like that."

Jean took Maggie's hand and led her past the rose bushes and various other plants that made up her lush garden. When they were out of sight of the house, Jean moved nearer to Maggie.

"I like you, Maggie Cranston."

"I like you, too, Jean."

Jean closed the distance between them. She stood taller than Maggie and looked into her eyes. The desire she saw matched her own. She slowly lowered her mouth until it was just inches from Maggie's.

"You're beautiful," Jean whispered.

She watched Maggie's eyes close. She brushed her lips lightly over Maggie's. They were soft and tasted faintly of martini. She pulled away.

"That was nice," she said.

"Very."

Jean kissed her again, more passionately this time. She ran her tongue over Maggie's lips and they parted, allowing her entry. Her mouth was warm and moist, much as she knew she'd find other parts. Her legs went weak as the kiss deepened.

"Come up to my room?" Jean whispered hoarsely.

"Lead the way."

Jean led Maggie in a secret entrance to avoid curious stares. She took her upstairs to her room. The big four-poster bed beckoned her. She kissed Maggie again, hard and powerfully, claiming her as her own.

As they kissed, Jean deftly unbuttoned Maggie's blouse. She slid it off her shoulders and down to the floor. The soft skin beneath the silky bra called to her. It teased her to the point of dizziness.

Lightheaded, she caressed the small mounds. She bent to kiss one, then the other.

"Please," Maggie murmured. "Get this off of me."

Jean reached around behind her and unhooked her bra. She tossed it to the floor, then held both breasts in her hands. She ran her thumbs over the pert nipples, and they stood hard under her touch. She lowered her head and licked one, feeling it harden even more. She sucked it deep in her mouth and felt the nipple pressed against the roof of her mouth.

Maggie held her head in place as she mewled. Jean was excited at the sounds she made. But she needed more. Much more.

While she continued to suck, Jean found the button and zipper to Maggie's skirt, and soon it joined the other clothes on the floor.

"My God, you're beautiful," Jean breathed.

She watched as the blush crept over every inch of Maggie. Her desire flared. She ran her hand down Maggie's backside and felt the satin fabric of her panties against her skin. She slipped her fingers inside the waistband and felt Maggie's stomach ripple in response. She knew Maggie was ripe for the picking and couldn't wait to taste her fruit.

Jean slid Maggie's panties off and watched her shapely legs as she stepped out of them. She eased her back on the bed. When she climbed on top, Maggie worked quickly to strip her clothes. Skin to skin, Jean kissed Maggie again, this time with all the pent up passion she had. She felt every inch of Maggie against her, her heated flesh spurring her on.

They continued kissing as they rubbed against each other. Jean finally broke the kiss and worked her way lower, once again taking a nipple in her mouth. She sucked on it, playfully at first, then in earnest. She was lost in the sensation of the hard nub in her mouth and the puckered areola against her lips.

She moved her hand to Maggie's other nipple and teased it. She twisted and tugged on it until Maggie cried out as she reached her first climax.

"You're amazing," Maggie said.

"I'm just getting started."

"Oh, my."

Jean continued to tease Maggie's nipples until she came again. She continued to suck on one while she slid her hand between Maggie's legs. She found her wet and ready for her.

"You feel so good," Jean said.

"So do you."

Jean stroked Maggie's swollen clit.

"You're so ready for me."

"That's an understatement."

Jean continued to stroke her until Maggie cried out again.

"You're killing me," Maggie said.

"But what a way to go, yes?"

Maggie spread her legs wider to allow Jean greater access. Jean dipped her fingers inside then dragged her juices all over her. She plunged her fingers deeper and deeper, massaging the satin walls and feeling them close around her.

She moved her mouth to Maggie's clit and drew it between her lips. She flicked her tongue over and under it. Maggie only lasted a few minutes before she screamed again.

"I can't take anymore," she said.

"You sure? Because I'm just getting warmed up."

"I'm sure. I can't."

Jean pulled Maggie close.

"You ready for some sleep?" she asked.

"Oh, no you don't. I get my turn now," Maggie said.

She rolled on top of Jean. She kissed down her chest, stopping briefly to lick a nipple. She continued her way down Jean's belly until she made herself comfortable between her legs. Maggie placed one of Jean's legs over her shoulder and gazed at her wet center.

"You're beautiful," she said.

She blew on Jean's hard clit.

"Oh, shit," Jean said. "Oh, God."

"You like that?"

"You're making me crazy."

"Good."

Maggie lowered her head and licked Jean's clit with a flat tongue. She lapped at it like a lollipop, and every pass made Jean's head spin faster.

"Oh, God. Don't stop."

Jean felt Maggie's teeth lightly scrape her and knew she wouldn't be able to last much longer. She closed her eyes and the colors burst behind her eyelids. She groaned as the orgasm washed over her.

Maggie continued to move her tongue along Jean until she was inside her.

"You taste divine," she said.

Her talented tongue continued to work its magic, and in no time, Jean was coming again.

Maggie snuggled next to Jean and they fell into a deep slumber.

CHAPTER TWO

Jean awoke the next morning to an empty bed. She looked around for a note or something, but found nothing. She quickly donned her housecoat and ran downstairs looking for Maggie. She was nowhere to be found.

Jean took in the disaster that was her house and was grateful that she had hired extra help for the day to clean it. There were plates and glasses everywhere, some with food and wine still in them. The scene added to her depression at Maggie's absence. If anyone left after a night of lovemaking, it was usually Jean. But she wouldn't have left Maggie. There was something different about her. Or so she thought.

Betty came around the corner as Jean stared at the mess.

"How are you today, Miss Sanders? You disappeared early last night."

"I did. I'm well today. Is anybody else here?" she asked hopefully.

"Just us, ma'am."

Jean hoped her disappointment didn't show.

"The others will be here to help you shortly though, yes?"

"They should be. And then may I take the day off tomorrow?"

"Certainly. And remember, you'll only need to come by three days a week while I'm gone."

"Yes, ma'am."

Jean walked up to her room with her head low. She was lonely already. It wasn't like her to feel this way the morning after. But the morning after usually meant more sex and then a quick good-bye. If there even was a morning after.

"Ma'am?"

She turned, unaware that Betty had followed her upstairs.

"Yes?"

"Do you need any help packing for your vacation?"

"Not right now. Perhaps later. For now, will you please run me a bath?"

"Gladly."

Jean stripped the sheets off her bed and put her travel bags on them. She should be more excited about her trip to Palm Springs, but she couldn't get Maggie out of her head. She smelled the subtle musk coming from the bathtub and found herself longing to indulge.

She walked into the bathroom and felt Betty's sure, strong hands on her shoulders.

"You're awfully tense this morning."

"I shouldn't be."

"No? Who was the lucky lady?"

"An up-and-comer. No one you've heard of. And you? How did you fare last night?"

"I was working, Miss Sanders. Though, Lord knows I was tempted."

"I'm sure you were. I'm surprised you were able to maintain your professionalism."

"It wasn't easy, to be sure. But I did it."

Betty slid Jean's housecoat off her shoulders.

"But I must say it left me quite randy."

Jean spun around and placed her hand between Betty's legs. She was dripping. Jean loved how she was always ready.

"Get out of that dress and join me in the tub."

Betty quickly obliged. Jean enjoyed the submissive role Betty played. It was a power trip for her to be able to order her around, and she only did it sexually. She would never treat her that way as an employer. But when it came to sex games, Jean was the mistress, and that role made her clit throb.

She watched Betty step out of her dress and stand before her in simply her stockings.

"You are such a good girl. No bra and no panties, just as I've instructed you."

Jean climbed into the tub and sank down to where her chin barely broke the water.

"What are you waiting for?" she asked. "I told you to get in the tub."

Betty placed a foot on the bathtub and unhooked her garter. Jean observed the process from an angle that gave her full view of Betty's wet pussy. By the time the other stocking was removed, Jean was quite sure she was about to explode.

Betty stepped in deliberately. She put one foot on the right side of Jean and one foot on the left. She stared down looking at Jean, who sat looking up at the pink heaven between Betty's legs.

"Kneel down," Jean commanded.

Betty dropped to one knee and then the other, rubbing herself against Jean's belly as she did so. Jean felt the slickness against her and closed her eyes. She needed to maintain control. Although all she wanted to do was stroke her own clit until she came.

With no pretense, Jean plunged her fingers deep inside Betty, who did nothing but squirm against them.

"You are so ready for me. Do you want me to fuck you, Betty? Beg me."

"Please, Mistress. Oh, please. Use me like the slut I am."

"I can do that. Get up on your knees."

Betty rose back to her knees. She reached out to caress one of Jean's breasts, the tip of which was barely visible above the sudsy water.

"Pinch my nipple," Jean said.

Betty complied. She pinched it hard while she twisted and pulled it.

"Holy fuck, that feels good. Don't stop. Rub my clit with your other hand."

It seemed like an eternity had passed and she didn't feel Betty's hand.

"Do it now, damn it!"

Her clit felt like it was six inches long. She needed it to be stroked while Betty had her way with her nipple. What was taking so long?

"Yes, Mistress."

Betty slipped her hand between Jean's legs and stroked her slick clit. Once, twice, three times, and Jean's world exploded into tiny fragments. As the pieces floated down and came back together, Jean was able to focus on Betty, nude in the tub with her.

"Lean back and spread your legs," Jean said.

Betty did as she was instructed. Betty's breasts were full and firm, and more than just their nipples showed above the water.

"Tease your tits for me," Jean said.

Betty played with her breasts. Not as hard and forcefully as she'd played with Jean's. She was tender and loving. She closed her eyes, apparently lost in the moment.

Jean reached out and closed her hands around Betty's. She made her squeeze her nipples much harder.

"Mistress, that hurts."

"But you've been a naughty bitch, haven't you?"

"No. I've been a good girl."

"How many women last night had their hands up your skirt?"

"But, Mistress, I was good."

"Define 'good,' you slut."

"I didn't encourage them or let them linger."

"In other words, you didn't let them get you off?"

"No, ma'am, I did not."

"But you want me to get you off, don't you?"

"Yes, ma'am. I always want that from you. Please, ma'am, my nipples really hurt."

Jean saw the tears leak out of Betty's eyes and realized she really was in pain.

"There, there," Jean said. "Your Mistress only wants you to know who's boss."

"I know you're the boss, Mistress. And if you need to punish me, I understand."

Jean looked down at Betty and saw how hard and puckered her nipples were. She might have been in pain, but clearly, she'd enjoyed it. Seeing them that shade of red turned Jean on anew. She leaned back in the tub.

"Fuck me again."

"But…" Betty began.

"But what?"

"Ma'am? When is it my turn?"

"When I say it's your turn. Now fuck me."

Betty choked back a sob. Jean knew how horny she must be. She knew her guests had teased her mercilessly the previous night. And now she was alone in the giant tub with her. She always took good care of her, but she wasn't being allowed to come. It had to make her crazy. Jean smiled. She was wetter than ever.

"Inside me, slut," Jean said.

Betty slipped four fingers inside Jean. Jean spread her legs wider and arched her hips to take her in. Jean met each thrust, over and over until she felt her insides clamp down around Betty as the orgasm tore through her.

Jean lay back against the tub, panting to catch her breath.

"That was wonderful," she said.

"I'm glad Mistress enjoyed it."

"Very much."

The suds had dissipated in the tub, and they were able to see each other through the water.

"Spread your legs for me," Jean said.

Betty did as she let out a little cry.

"What's wrong?" Jean asked.

"Please, Mistress. May I come? Will you make me come?"

"I will when I'm ready. For now, show me your pussy."

Betty pulled her outer lips back and showed off her bright pink pussy to Jean. Jean could see how wet she was.

"I can see your cream from here."

"Will you touch me, Mistress?"

"When I'm ready. Now touch yourself."

Jean fought not to stroke her own clit as she watched Betty. She saw her large clit and swollen lips grow as her fingers danced over them. She looked up at Betty's face and saw her eyes begin to close.

"I need you again. Now," Jean said.

"What?" Betty sounded like she'd been woken up.

"I need you. Get over here."

"But..."

"But what? You don't deny your Mistress. Get over here now."

Jean knew she was being particularly cruel, but didn't care. She knew when she finally did allow Betty to come, it would be one of the most powerful orgasms she'd ever had.

Betty crawled across the tub and slipped her fingers inside Jean again. She pulled them out and dragged them over her clit.

Jean leaned her head against the tub and closed her eyes. Nothing in the world mattered except Betty's magical fingers. She was close. The darkness crept in from the side until everything was black. Then the lights happened again. Bright streaks of lights lit up her eyelids.

When she was able to function, she opened her eyes in time to see Betty stroking herself frantically.

"What do you think you're doing?" Jean asked. "Who told you you could touch yourself?"

"Please, Mistress. Please."

"Stop!"

Betty stopped what she was doing and looked at Jean. Jean could see the begging in her eyes.

"Don't you ever touch yourself without my permission."

"I'm sorry. I can't help myself. Please touch me now."

Jean leaned over and kissed Betty. She ran her hands over Betty's breast, lightly teasing her this time. She kissed her hard and ran her hand down her body, finding her so wet she couldn't resist her any longer.

She slipped her fingers inside her and stroked her hard and fast. She felt amazing and tight.

"Oh, God, Betty. You feel so good."

It didn't take any time for Betty to cry out. It was an earth-shattering scream as she finally reached the climax she'd been denied for so long.

"Oh, my God. Thank you, Mistress."

"You're quite welcome. Now get dressed and get my suitcases. I need to pack when I get out of the bath.

Jean leaned back and lit a cigarette. She wondered anew where Maggie had disappeared to. Betty was fun, but she was the help. There was something about Maggie that really called to her.

"Would you like me to start packing for you?" Betty asked.

"No, thank you. Leave the bags on the bed. I'll pack. You'd better get started on this house."

"Yes, ma'am."

Jean watched appreciatively as Betty walked away. She crushed out her cigarette and got out of the bath. After toweling off, she opened one of her walk-in closets. She chose a long blue skirt and a white button down shirt with a collar. How she hated skirts and dresses, but she knew to be seen in pants would be scandalous for her.

After dressing, she packed her bags. Lightweight, summery clothes would be appropriate for a week in Palm Springs. Being on hiatus from filming meant she had time to vacation. And she knew one of the places to see and be seen was Palm Springs, vacation spot of the stars. So she would go, see the sights, enjoy the hot springs, and maybe get lucky, which was always one of her goals.

David picked her up an hour later in his Cadillac. The trip only took a couple of hours, and soon they were checking in to La Mirage. At the desk, Jean was greeted by no less than twenty other movie stars. She was hugged and kissed and welcomed to the warm, dry desert.

She agreed to meet Arthur Langdon at three o'clock for tennis and drinks following. She didn't mind, really. He was a nice man, not a groper like so many of them were. She'd probably enjoy the time with him.

"You're so lucky to have a date with Arthur." David swooned as she unpacked. "He's the cat's meow."

"I don't consider it a date," Jean said.

"Oh, come now. It's a date, dear."

Jean thought about it. She supposed it could be construed as a date, but she didn't think of it that way, obviously.

"Maybe it is. I don't know. It doesn't matter."

"If it was me on a date with him, he'd have the time of his life."

Jean simply looked at David. She supposed Arthur Langdon was an attractive man. He was tall and fit with blue eyes and jet-black hair.

"Well, I'm sorry he asked me out instead of you," Jean said.

"Me, too."

"So what will you do to occupy yourself while I play tennis?"

"I'll find something to do. Maybe plead chaperone so I can watch your tennis match and get to enjoy drinks with you two."

"If you must," Jean said. "I have no problem with that."

"Oh, thank you!" He hugged Jean. "I need to go choose an appropriate outfit. I'll see you just before three."

Jean set about unpacking and settling in. She was relaxing on the chaise lounge when David knocked on her door.

"Jean? Darling? Are you ready?"

Jean opened the door and stepped out into the hallway.

"David, dear, could those shorts be any shorter?" she asked.

"No reason not to advertise, love."

"Well, I wish I was wearing them. This skirt is entirely too revealing."

"Poor dear. It's the world we live in. We must adhere to the norms or risk our careers."

"I know. That doesn't mean I have to like it."

They found their way to the tennis courts and saw Arthur relaxing at a table with a cocktail. He rose as they approached.

"Hello again, Jean." He kissed her on her cheek.

"Hello, Arthur. Do you know David Duvall?"

"Sure. We've worked together before." He shook David's hand.

Jean glanced at David and saw the blush on his cheeks. She hoped Arthur hadn't noticed.

"Shall we?" Arthur motioned to the tennis racquets.

"Sure," Jean said.

They played well together and seemed to be evenly matched, though something told Jean Arthur was going easy on her. She didn't mind. The exercise felt good, and Jean was sorry when the game ended.

They walked to the bar together.

"So what's Duvall's story?" Arthur asked.

Jean felt a flutter in her stomach. Was he interested? Or was he the enemy?

"What do you mean?"

"I mean, why is he with you?"

"He's my chaperone this trip."

"Oh, that's very chivalrous of him."

"David's a good guy," Jean said.

They joined David at the bar and each ordered a drink. Conversation was light and pleasant at first, then Arthur mentioned something disturbing.

"Are you two familiar with Thomas O'Leary?"

"I haven't heard of him," Jean said. "Is he a new actor?"

"He's not," David said. "I've heard of him. He's a little scary."

"He's not scary," Arthur said. "He wants to get all the pinkos and fags out of Hollywood. Nothing wrong with that."

"He's just the boogeyman," David said. "I don't think anything will come of it."

"What have you got to be afraid of?" Arthur asked.

"Nothing. I just don't think he'll be able to do all that he says he will."

"I suppose we'll just have to wait and see," Arthur said.

"Surely we can find something more enjoyable to talk about," Jean said.

"Sure. I just find politics fascinating," Arthur said. "But perhaps we can talk about dinner instead. I'd love to take you out tonight."

Jean fought the familiar nausea that came when a man asked her out. She knew if she said no to one of Hollywood's most eligible bachelors, tongues would wag.

"I'd like that."

"And, David, I'm sure you can find something to do while I wine and dine the lady? Trust me, she'll be in good hands."

"I've no doubt she will. I'll keep myself busy while you have dinner."

"Great. Meet me in the lobby, say seven o'clock?"

"I'll be there," Jean said.

Chapter Three

Jean rode back to her suite with David.

"What an ass," David said.

"He is."

"And you're having dinner with him."

"What was I supposed to do? Tell him I'm gay?"

"No, and shhh. I'm sure the elevators have ears."

"Not you and this O'Leary guy again."

"I don't know, Jean. What if it happens? What if they kick us all out of Hollywood?"

"Then who's going to make the movies? Answer me that, David. It will never happen."

She got off the elevator with a promise to call David in the morning.

She laid out her clothes for the evening on the bed. She chose a red cocktail dress. She would look bright and cheerful, which was completely opposite of how she'd feel.

Oh, well, she told herself as she got in the shower. It wasn't the first time she'd done this and it wouldn't be the last. It was just dinner and she could handle that.

She showered and dressed and was in the downstairs lobby fashionably late at ten after seven. There was no sign of Arthur.

She found that rude, but sat and waited for him. He showed up five minutes later and greeted her with a kiss on the cheek.

"I apologize for my tardiness. I got a call from my studio."

"Oh. Good news, I hope?"

"Very. They set me up for a reading for a big new movie. I'm not to discuss details, but trust me, I'm very excited."

"Well then, I'm excited for you."

Arthur offered his elbow, which Jean slipped her hand through. He led her to the grand dining room. Chandeliers hung from the ceiling, but they were muted and the atmosphere was subdued and, Jean thought, perhaps romantic with the right person.

During the appetizer, Jean heard all about how successful Arthur was. He droned on and on about all his successes. Jean found it hard not to yawn on several occasions.

"We should make a movie together," Arthur said.

"What? Why do you say that?" Jean was suddenly awake and paying attention.

"Well, you're America's Sweetheart, and I'm their favorite leading man. Together we'd make magic on the silver screen."

"I suppose that would be true. And who knows? Maybe someday we will star together."

"Maybe on this big new movie. I'll recommend you to my studio to read for the leading lady."

"I'm sure if it's that big of a part, the studio will get me a reading." Jean hoped she didn't sound ungrateful, but she didn't want Arthur thinking she needed his help getting a role. She held Hollywood in the palm of her hand and could get whatever part she wanted.

"I hope so. I'd sure like to star opposite you." He reached out and took her hand.

She saw the flash go off before she could pull her hand away. There were more flashes and she smiled, knowing pictures of Arthur Langdon holding her hand would be all over the papers in the morning. Nothing could help her more in keeping up her façade.

However, she didn't appreciate his familiarity and so withdrew her hand.

"Damn movie rags. They'll turn that into the story of the century," Arthur said.

"Nobody believes those old things anyway," Jean lied.

"Are you kidding me? People hang on every word that's printed in those."

Jean laughed.

"Oh, well. Let them talk."

"You really don't mind?"

"I couldn't care less what the press says," Jean said.

"But you live such a private life. I always assumed you hated the press."

"I would hate them if they invaded said private life, but when I'm in public, I'm fair game. Especially in a place like this. It's teeming with movie stars. They're bound to end up with inaccurate pictures and quotes taken out of context. It's just something we have to accept."

"Well, now that they've seen us together, I doubt they'll leave us alone."

"That's only if they see us together again. It's really nothing to worry about," Jean said.

"I'm glad you feel that way. But I would like to see you again, so it may be a problem."

"I'm only here for a week and there are so many people to see and so much to do," Jean said. "I'd like to see you again, too, but I don't know that it will happen."

"That being the case, we should make the most out of tonight. Shall we dance after dinner?"

The game was the same, but there was something about Arthur that made Jean decidedly uncomfortable. She told herself she was being ridiculous.

"That would be lovely."

Dinner continued with Arthur rambling on about how wonderful he was and Jean pretending to care. He wasn't half the star she was, but she acted like he was. Sure, he had the looks, but the talent was sorely lacking. She didn't dare tell him that, though.

After dinner, Arthur escorted Jean to the ballroom where they danced the night away. Jean was in his arms when she felt someone's gaze on her. She turned to see a beautiful woman only a few years older than her watching her as she moved in the arms of her own partner. The look the woman gave Jean told her she'd much rather be dancing with her.

She begged off the next dance, pleading thirst. Arthur went to get her a drink, and the woman crossed the floor to Jean.

"Hello," she said in a deep, husky voice.

"Hello," Jean said.

"I've been watching you. You're quite a dancer."

"Thank you. So are you."

"I'd love to take a turn with you around the floor," the woman said.

"I think I'd enjoy that, too."

"Meet me in my room at midnight. We'll dance together. I'm in seventeen thirty-five."

"I'll be there."

It was late when Jean told Arthur she was tired and told him she wanted to go up to her rooms.

"I'll escort you, of course," Arthur said.

As soon as the elevator doors were closed, Arthur pulled Jean close and kissed her hard on her mouth, forcing his tongue inside.

Jean fought the urge to gag as she tried to push him off.

He finally broke the kiss and was moving in for another, but Jean deftly turned her head to the side.

"I don't know what you take me for, Mr. Langdon. But I am not that kind of girl."

"Aw, come on. We had a swell time. Don't be that way."

"I don't know what way you think I'm being, but I'm a decent lady and I'll not be manhandled."

Arthur straightened up.

"I apologize. I lost my head. It's just you're so beautiful and I really like you."

"Then show me some respect."

"I will."

They arrived at her suite and she stepped off the elevator.

"Until next time, Mr. Langdon."

"Good night, Jean."

Jean let herself in her suite and quickly stripped out of her cocktail dress. She slipped on a pair of white slacks and a yellow shirt. She checked herself out in the mirror. Yes, definitely more her style.

She poured herself a drink to calm her nerves. Both Arthur's attack and the anticipation of meeting the stranger had her nerves on edge. The drink would help.

Soon it was midnight and she took the elevator to the seventeenth floor. She found seventeen thirty-five and knocked on the door. She could hear music playing quietly inside. Her crotch twitched. This could prove to be a wonderful night after all.

The woman opened the door dressed similarly to Jean, in slacks and a shirt. The green of the shirt made her brown eyes sparkle.

"Please come in," she said.

Jean entered and looked around. The room was nice, but not as nice as her suite, of course. There was a bed along the far wall and a sofa along the side wall. A phonograph just to her left was playing music.

"I don't travel without my records."

"I like your taste in music."

"Thank you."

"Would you like to dance?"

"I would."

Jean moved into the woman's arms and felt uncomfortable. She wasn't sure who should lead. Leading felt natural for her, but this woman seemed used to being in charge. She was right. The woman took her and held her close as she squired her around the room.

"Isn't this better than your earlier partner?" the woman asked.

"Much."

Jean relaxed and let the woman and music guide her. Soon she was lost in the feelings of the woman's body against her and the soft, slow rhythm of the music. She knew nothing about this woman and assumed she knew nothing about her either. She didn't even know the woman's name. Somehow that added to the wonderment. This could make for a magical night.

Jean wanted nothing more than a little fun. She wasn't sure what the woman's intentions were though. Sure, they'd dance, but Jean definitely felt the need for more. She looked into the woman's eyes and saw the depth of passion that burned there.

She looked down at her mouth and saw the woman's lips parted slightly, inviting her for a kiss.

As she watched, the woman flicked her tongue out and wet her lips. Jean couldn't have resisted if she tried. She lowered her mouth and tasted the woman's. It was soft and sweet and Jean wanted more.

The record stopped and the woman stepped away. Jean wondered if she'd done something wrong.

"How about a drink? I have a bottle of champagne chilling."

"Champagne would be nice."

The woman expertly uncorked the bottle and filled two flutes. They sat together on the couch. Jean put her arm around the woman.

"So what brings you to Palm Springs?" she asked.

"The bathhouses. I love the hot springs here. I love to soak in them. I feel reborn after that, you know?"

"I do know. Shame it's not earlier. I'd suggest a soak tonight."

"I have other plans tonight," the woman said.

Jean's heart sank.

"You do?"

"I thought we did," the woman said.

"We do indeed," Jean said.

She took the woman's champagne and set it on the table. She leaned in for another kiss. This one was less tentative, yet she still held back. The woman kissed her back with the same need.

"Come." The woman stood. "Let's dance some more."

Jean moved back into her arms and allowed herself to be led once more around the room. This time, when they passed the bed, the woman eased Jean down onto it.

"Isn't this more like it?" she asked.

"It is if you join me."

The woman lowered herself on top of Jean. She kissed her hard on the mouth, her tongue pressing against Jean's lips, demanding entrance. Jean was happy to oblige. She opened her mouth and welcomed the soft, firm tongue. She danced around it, chasing it through her mouth as the woman searched her mouth with it.

Jean was breathless when the kiss ended.

The woman brushed Jean's hair back off her face.

"You are a very attractive woman. And you look so much more relaxed in these slacks than you did in that dress earlier. It's not often I find a woman like me who I really find attractive. Fate surely brought us together for this night."

Jean swallowed hard. One night with this woman. That's all the woman wanted and all she would get. It was all either of them would need.

The woman pinned Jean's hands above her head and kissed her neck.

"You taste so good," she said.

She unbuttoned Jean's shirt quickly and efficiently. She bit down on the exposed breasts above her bra.

"Ouch," Jean said, more out of surprise than actual pain.

"Did that really hurt?" the woman asked.

"I suppose not."

"Good. Because I'd hate to think we've come this far only to have to say good night."

"No, definitely not."

"Are you afraid of me?" the woman asked.

"No."

She ripped Jean's bra off and tossed it to the side.

"Now?"

"Maybe a little," Jean admitted.

"No reason to fear me. Just relax and we'll have some fun." She closed her teeth over one of Jean's nipples. Hard enough for it to hurt, but not so hard that it wasn't pleasurable.

"I knew you'd be fun the minute I saw you," the woman said.

She bit down on the other nipple.

"Stay here," she said. She walked to the chest of drawers and came back.

She had two clothespin looking things in her hands. She clamped one on each of Jean's nipples. Jean squirmed at the discomfort even as she marveled at the level of arousal she was achieving.

"Too much?" the woman asked.

"Not yet," Jean answered. She wondered how far the woman would go. And how much she could take.

"Excellent," the woman said.

She pinned Jean's hands above her head again and this time tied them together with a scarf. She looped the other end of the scarf around the headboard and tied it.

Jean felt helpless. It was a feeling she was quite unaccustomed to, but she found she liked it. It was nice letting someone else call the shots for a change.

The woman quickly unzipped Jean's slacks and deftly pulled them off. She climbed between Jean's legs, which Jean spread willingly. She felt something hard and buzzing against her thigh. She felt herself grow wet. Soon she was throbbing. She needed something and needed it soon.

She felt the vibrator slide up her inner leg and opened her legs wider. The tip pulsated against her opening. She wanted to cry out, to beg for the woman to slide it inside her, but she didn't. She held her tongue.

The woman moved the toy so it pressed against Jean's clit. Electricity coursed through Jean's veins. She arched her hips for more contact. The woman pressed harder. Jean cried out as she climaxed.

She hadn't even caught her breath when the woman moved the vibrator inside her. She buried it deep, as deep as it would go. Jean had never felt so full. The woman slowly moved it out and then back in. Slowly at first, then faster, the woman plunged the toy in and out of Jean. Jean's head moved back and forth on the pillow as she absorbed each plunge. Each thrust took her closer and closer to the brink.

"Do you want to come?" the woman asked.

"Yes."

"Tell me."

"I want to come," Jean said.

"I don't believe you."

"I need to come. Please," Jean said.

"How bad?"

"I'm desperate," Jean said. "I need to come. I need to come now."

The woman slowly removed the toy and slid it back in, running the tip along one of Jean's satin walls. Jean had never felt anything like it. She closed her eyes tight and screamed as she came over and over again.

Jean was exhausted by the time the woman was through with her. She was satiated like she'd never been. She lay back like a bowl of Jell-O. She couldn't even move.

The woman untied Jean's arms. Jean rubbed her wrists. She hadn't even noticed how numb her arms had become.

Next, the woman took the clamps off Jean's nipples.

Jean breathed a sigh of relief.

"Aren't those fun?" the woman asked.

"They really are. I might have to invest in some."

"I highly recommend them."

The woman picked Jean's clothes off the floor and handed them to her.

"Here you go. You may get dressed now."

"What about you?" Jean asked, longing for a chance to please the woman's beautiful body.

"Oh, no. I wanted you. You don't get me. It's one of my rules."

"But surely you have needs." Jean stepped toward the woman and placed her hands on her chest.

The woman gripped her wrists hard.

"I said no," she said.

"Okay." Jean backed away. "I just thought we could keep the fun going."

"I've had my fun. It's time for you to leave. Now."

Jean dressed quickly and headed for the door.

"I did have fun," the woman said. "You were amazing."

"As were you."

"Thank you for agreeing to meet me."

"It was my pleasure."

"Good night, then."

"Good night," Jean said and let herself out of the room.

Chapter Four

The following day, David escorted Jean to the bathhouses. He left her at the women's house with the admonishment that he'd be back in one hour. Jean appreciated that. The hot springs were wonderful, and she would spend all day there if she could. But they weren't healthy in those kinds of doses, so she would listen to David.

She went into the dressing room and stripped out of her clothes. She donned a thick white robe and walked toward the sulfur-scented tubs. She took off her robe and stepped into the hot water. She immediately felt the healing qualities working on her.

As she sank in, she closed her eyes and pondered the past few days. Life was strange, indeed. Though, she was having fun, to be sure. She wondered what was in store for her over the rest of her stay in Palm Springs.

"Hi, Jean. Remember me?" a woman from the next tub over said.

"I'm sorry. You look familiar, but I can't place you."

"I met you at the party you threw the other night. I was there with Dorothy Martin."

"Ah, yes. Well, good to see you again." Jean closed her eyes again.

"How long are you in Palm Springs for?" the woman asked.

Jean opened her eyes again. Clearly, she'd get no peace while this woman was there. The woman was very attractive, though, so it might be worth giving her some time.

"I'm here for the week. And you?"

"We're here for the week, as well. We should get together."

"Who's 'we'?" Jean asked.

"Dorothy and myself."

Jean felt her clit twitch. This almost proved that Dorothy was a lesbian. She had a woman as a date for Jean's party and the same woman accompanied her to Palm Springs. Maybe Jean had a shot at bedding Dorothy, after all.

"I'd like that," Jean said. "Why not meet for cocktails this afternoon? Say four o'clock?"

"That would work perfectly," the woman said. "We're staying at La Mirage."

"As am I. I'll meet you two in the bar then."

"Sounds swell."

The woman got out of her tub and Jean watched appreciatively as the water rivulets trickled down her body. She had a fantastic figure, with large breasts and hips. Just what Jean looked for in a woman. Jean felt herself getting wet.

When the woman was gone, Jean closed her eyes and thought of the promise of the evening ahead. She relaxed in the warm water, but not completely. Part of her was too excited at the prospects that lay ahead.

David met her out in front of the baths precisely one hour after he'd dropped her off. She was all smiles.

"What got into you in those tubs?" David asked. "Or do I want to know?"

"I have a date for drinks today with the luscious Dorothy Martin."

"Oh, dear. Jean, please be careful."

"Don't be silly, David. I'm the most discreet person you'll ever meet."

"I certainly hope so. But the press is all over down here. I'd hate for you to meet your ruin because you can't keep your hormones in check."

"Oh, David." She looped her arm through his elbow. "How you worry. And for nothing."

David arched an eyebrow at her.

"Well, what am I to do while you work your magic on Miss Martin?"

"Anything you want. I'm sure you can find a hunk to spend the time with."

"I certainly enjoyed chaperoning you and Arthur Langdon yesterday, speaking of hunks."

Jean shuddered.

"What?"

"The man tried to force himself on me last night. It was repulsive."

"You mean he—?"

"Oh, no. Not that far. He just tried to kiss me in a manner I'd prefer no man kiss me."

"I'm sorry, Jean. I sure wish I'd have been you. I would have enjoyed it immensely."

"I hate to break it to you, but I don't think you're his type."

David sighed.

"Perhaps not, but there's plenty more eye candy here to enjoy."

"And I do hope you'll enjoy it to the full extent."

"By the way." David handed Jean a copy of the national celebrity rag. "Speaking of you and Arthur Langdon."

Jean stared down at the picture of the two of them holding hands at the restaurant. She followed the instructions and turned to page ten for more of the story. There were pictures of them dancing. She smiled.

"How could anyone think I was a lesbian after spending such an obviously wonderful evening with America's leading man?"

"And what a man he is," David said.

They wandered back to the hotel and said their good-byes so Jean could get ready for drinks. She showered and chose a suitable outfit to meet the others. She wore a beige, ankle-length skirt and a purple shirt. Conservative, but not overly so. And masculine enough to send the right message to Dorothy, in case she was wondering.

She arrived at the bar at precisely four o'clock to find Dorothy and her companion already there. Dorothy stood when Jean walked up.

"Jean Sanders, it's been too long."

She pulled Jean into an embrace.

"It truly has. Though I heard you were at my party the other night, I never saw you."

"I was there. What a wonderful party it was, too, my dear. You are quite a hostess."

"Why, thank you."

Dorothy turned slightly.

"And of course, you've met my assistant, Mary."

"Not officially," Jean said. She wondered what sort of assistant Mary was. A personal assistant? If so, then why would she have accompanied Dorothy to the party? It made no sense to Jean. She was sure they were lovers.

"Then, allow me to introduce you. Jean Sanders, this is Mary Bedford. Mary, Jean Sanders."

Jean shook Mary's hand.

"It's nice to have a name to go with the person now," Jean said.

"May I buy you a drink?" Dorothy said.

"Sure. I'll take a bourbon," Jean said.

Jean took a sip of her bourbon and glanced around the room. There were quite a few people in the room. Many of them were movie and radio stars. Jean loved rubbing shoulders with other dignitaries of Hollywood. Many times it was trying for her to keep up her façade, but other times it was a heady feeling.

Her gaze landed on the beautiful figure of a woman facing away from her. She had long brown hair and shapely legs. Jean thought of Maggie. When the woman turned and Jean saw her silhouette, she knew it was indeed Maggie.

"Excuse me," she said to Dorothy and Mary. She crossed the room to Maggie and placed a hand on her shoulder.

"Maggie?" she said.

Maggie turned and smiled.

"Hello, Jean."

"Can we talk?" Jean said.

"Certainly." She excused herself from her group of friends. "It's good to see you. And very surprising that you remember me."

"Why? I wasn't drunk or anything that night."

"I know. But I'm still a nobody in what I'm sure is a string of nobodies for you."

"I'm not that way," Jean said. "Well, not exactly."

Maggie grinned.

"Not exactly, huh?"

"I do have an active libido, I'll admit. But that's not the point. Why did you leave? I woke up the next morning and you were gone."

"I didn't want any awkward morning after. I thought it would be best if I was gone when you woke up."

"Well, I didn't like that. I missed you."

"That's very sweet of you," Maggie said. "But you have to admit, it saved us both that embarrassment that follows a night of anonymous sex."

"Maybe you're right. But I wanted more of it when I woke up and was very disappointed that you were gone."

"I'm sorry, then. More of that would have been wonderful."

"Join me for dinner tonight," Jean said.

"Do you think that's a good idea?" Maggie said. "People would talk."

"People would see an up-and-coming star having dinner with America's Sweetheart. They'd assume I'm sharing with you tricks of the trade. I think it would appear perfectly natural."

"I'm not sure."

"Please, Maggie. Six o'clock in the lobby. I'll meet you there. I need to get back to my party now. But please say you'll meet me."

"I'll meet you. You have more to lose than I do, so if you think it's safe, I'll be there."

"Very well. I'll see you at six."

She made her way back to Dorothy and Mary who were whispering to each other.

"Am I interrupting?" Jean asked.

"Not at all," Dorothy said. "Who's your friend?"

"Oh, she's an up-and-coming actress I met the other night. I've agreed to have dinner with her tonight so she can pick my brain."

"That's so nice of you, Miss Sanders," Mary said.

"Please call me Jean."

Mary flushed and Jean smiled.

"That really is nice of you, Jean," Dorothy said. "Sometimes young starlets can be so trying. They think they have what it takes when they'll never make it, and yet you have to be encouraging and make them think they have a chance."

"This woman seems to be moving up the ranks," Jean said. "I don't mind helping her out if I can."

The afternoon passed in pleasant conversation, but Jean wasn't fully attentive. She was drinking with Dorothy Martin, her ultimate fantasy, but her mind was on Maggie. She didn't understand, but she couldn't stop.

Six o'clock arrived and Jean excused herself to meet up with Maggie.

She found Maggie waiting in the lobby. She was dressed in a green cocktail dress that showed off her green eyes. Jean's breath caught at the sight of her. She wanted her again at that moment, but knew she'd have to be discreet. David was right. She needed to play it safe.

"Tell me about yourself," Jean said after the waiter poured the wine.

"What do you want to know? I told you last time that I'm an actress."

"I know you went to Bryn Mawr, but what about before then?"

"I grew up in Pottsville. It's a small town in Pennsylvania."

"I've never heard of it."

"No one has," Maggie said.

"What did your parents do?" Jean said.

"My mother died in childbirth, so I never knew her."

"I'm sorry."

"Thank you. But I came to terms with it a long time ago."

"Still, it had to be hard growing up without a mother," Jean said.

"My father was a good man. He took good care of me growing up."

"You say that past tense. Is he gone?"

"No. He disowned me when he found out I wanted to be an actress."

"I'm sorry."

"That's okay," Maggie said. "But it taught me you can't trust anyone to be there for you."

"That's a bit of a harsh generalization," Jean said.

Maggie shrugged.

"It's true. People only hurt you."

"I'm sorry you feel that way."

"I'm sorry," Maggie said. "I don't mean to put a damper on our dinner."

"It's okay. Let's just not dwell on that. What did your father do?"

"He was a city council member for many years. He was also a lawyer."

"Sounds like a real stand up guy."

"Well, he was a bit of a womanizer," Maggie said. "I guess you and he had that in common."

"You certainly don't have a very high opinion of me. I don't know why you think I'm a womanizer. Quite the contrary."

"It was obvious you were on the prowl at your party."

Jean laughed.

"It was, was it? I simply thought I was enjoying myself."

"I watched you for quite a while before I approached you," Maggie said.

"Well, I must say, I'm very glad you approached me. I really enjoyed myself that night."

"As did I."

"But you must understand, in my position, I couldn't afford to be a womanizer even if I wanted to be." Jean knew she wasn't being honest, but also felt that if Maggie would be hers, she could end her womanizing ways.

"I admit, I wondered how you kept your reputation so clean."

"My career depends on it."

"I suppose it does. And now mine does, too."

"It will. You'll need to be careful."

"I will."

"May I see you tonight?" Jean lowered her voice.

"What do you mean?"

"You know what I mean. Come to my room tonight."

"Jean, that's dangerous. I won't risk it."

"Please. I need you."

Maggie stood.

"Thank you for dinner. It was wonderful. Perhaps our paths will cross again."

Jean sat dumbfounded as Maggie walked out.

She couldn't believe Maggie had turned her down. She didn't know what it was about Maggie, but she couldn't get her out of her head. And now that she knew Maggie had trouble trusting people, she felt driven to prove Maggie could trust her. She took a deep breath. She'd see Maggie again. Of this, she was certain.

Jean wandered back to the bar, hoping to find solitude. Instead, she found a tipsy Dorothy and Mary.

"Have you been here the whole time?" she asked.

"We have," Dorothy said. "We've been having a gay old time. How was dinner?"

"It was fine. I gave her a few tips. I'm sure she was happy."

"Again, I have to say how gracious that was of you."

"That's nice of you to say," Jean said.

"We were just getting ready to head back to our suite," Dorothy said. "Would you care to join us for drinks up there?"

Jean gazed hard into Dorothy's eyes. What she saw there made her crotch clench. She swore she saw a longing that matched her own. A chance with Dorothy Martin was not something she was willing to pass up. Not after striking out with Maggie. But how did Mary fit in?

"Sure. That'd be swell."

They took the elevator up to their suite. Jean noticed how close Mary stood to Dorothy. She was certain they were lovers. So the question was really how did she fit in?

She tried to quell her libido. She told herself she was just going up for drinks. But she wanted with all she was for more to happen. She had desired Dorothy since the first time she laid eyes on her. She would play it cool and follow their lead. If nothing happened, she'd just have to take matters into her own hands when she got back to her suite.

They arrived at Dorothy's suite. Mary walked to the phonograph and turned it on. Dorothy made them each a drink. She handed one to Jean. Their fingers touched, and Jean felt the electricity. The touch lingered and Jean fought to catch her breath.

"Thank you," Jean said when she found her voice.

"You're welcome. Come over here and sit next to me."

Jean sat with her. She looked around and didn't see Mary.

"Where did Mary go?" she asked.

"She'll be right with us," Dorothy said. "So tell me, what's your next project?"

"I don't have one lined up right now. I told my studio not to line any scripts up for me until after I get back from Palm Springs."

They chatted about movies they'd been in and ones they'd been fortunate enough not to. They talked about which directors were tolerable to work for and which ones were just frustrated queens.

Their conversation was interrupted when a door opened and Mary danced out wearing a red satin negligee and red stiletto heels. She made her way over to Dorothy and wrapped her arms around her neck as she gyrated her hips in time with the music.

Jean felt like a voyeur, but couldn't look away. Mary obviously knew what she was doing, and Dorothy seemed somewhat pleased, if not overly so. Jean knew if a woman danced like that for her, she'd never be able to keep her hands to herself. Yet Dorothy sat there, eyes showing appreciation, but her body remained rigid.

Mary danced away from Dorothy. She moved to the center of the floor and danced to the music. Arms above her head, body swaying back and forth, she put on a show that Jean was more than happy to watch.

She wondered again why she'd been invited. Until Mary danced over to her. She spread her legs above Jean's and danced down until she was grinding against her. Jean felt her wet pussy pressed into her.

Jean put her hands on Mary's thighs. They were soft and supple, while muscular at the same time. She wasn't sure what she was allowed to do, but she longed to run her hands all over the beautiful body in front of her.

Mary stood and danced away from Jean, moving once again in the center of the floor. Jean felt Dorothy's gaze on her. She looked over at her. Dorothy smiled.

"She's good, isn't she?"

"Very," Jean said.

Mary danced back to Dorothy. This time she kissed her neck and ran her hands through Dorothy's hair. All the while, she seemed lost in the music.

Dorothy gently pushed Mary away, toward Jean. Mary took one of Jean's hands and pressed it to her breast. She writhed against her.

"Kiss me," Mary whispered. "Please kiss me."

Jean placed her hands on Mary's cheeks and pulled her mouth to her. Mary opened her mouth and encouraged Jean to dart her tongue inside. Jean was happy to oblige. She was getting wetter by the second, even as she was still slightly confused as to the outcome of the evening.

While Jean continued to kiss Mary, she caught movement out of the corner of her eye. It was Dorothy, who had sidled up behind Mary and wrapped her hands around her. Dorothy's hand was on Jean's hand on Mary's breast, and Jean thought she would explode at the contact.

Jean was in a fog as Mary was pulled away from her and Dorothy's mouth replaced Mary's on hers. Dorothy Martin was kissing her. Her head spun with pent up passion. She pulled Dorothy closer, still unsure of the rules, but caring less what they might be with each passing second.

Dorothy kissed her harder, almost bruising Jean's lips. Jean didn't care. She cared for nothing but the promise of what lay ahead.

"Do you want me?" Dorothy said.

"Yes."

"Do you want Mary?"

It took Jean a moment to register that Mary was still there.

"Is this a choice I have to make?"

"Not at all." Mary was suddenly standing with them, naked. Her breasts pressed against their faces.

Jean turned and greedily took a breast in her mouth. She heard Mary gasp. Or was it Dorothy? She didn't care. The breast was too beautiful to leave untouched.

"That's right," Dorothy said. "Enjoy her body. She's here for our enjoyment."

"What about you?" Jean said.

"Oh, I'm here for you, too. And believe me, you're here for me."

"I like the sound of that." Jean went back to suckling Mary. She heard the smack and felt Mary jump.

"What's going on?" she asked.

"Mary's not doing a good job. You and I are both fully clothed. She needs to take care of that."

Mary bent over Jean, her breasts swaying just out of reach as she unbuttoned her shirt. She slipped it off her. Next, she pressed her breasts into Jean as she reached around her to unhook her bra.

Jean was getting hotter with each passing moment. She felt like she might implode. She was a throbbing, wet mess.

Mary buried her face between Jean's breasts while she unbuttoned her skirt. She kissed her belly as she unzipped her skirt. When the skirt was lying in a heap on the floor, Mary knelt between Jean's legs. She spread them wide and pressed her face to her.

"Holy Jesus," Jean said. Never had she felt such a talented tongue on her. She closed her eyes as she teetered toward the precipice.

She heard the smack and Mary stopped. Jean swallowed hard. She gripped the armrests of her chair. She wanted to beg

Dorothy to please let Mary finish, but when she could finally focus on Dorothy, she saw that she meant business.

"I'm still dressed. No treats for you until all of us are naked. Now, kiss me."

Dorothy ran her tongue all over the inside of Mary's mouth. She looked at Jean.

"You taste delicious."

"Thank you. I have to say, that Mary is quite good."

"Oh, Jean. The night is young. You have no idea what talents the girl truly has."

Jean glanced at Mary's ass and saw the distinct red marks left by Dorothy. She wondered how bad they hurt. It didn't seem to bother Mary as she began to undress her mistress. Dorothy slipped her fingers inside Mary, who bit her lip to keep from crying out. Jean watched as Dorothy thrust in and out. She saw Mary move against her as she tried to focus on removing Dorothy's clothes.

She saw Mary's legs begin to quiver.

"Don't you come, girl," Dorothy said. "Don't you dare come yet."

Mary cried softly and, with shaky hands, continued to undress Dorothy. When Dorothy was naked, she pulled her fingers out of Mary. Jean knew just how Mary felt. She, too, had been so close to the edge when Dorothy ordered Mary to stop pleasing her.

"You sit here, Mary," Dorothy said. "Jean and I will go get comfortable on the bed. And Mary? Don't you dare touch yourself."

Dorothy stood looking at Mary as if contemplating her next move.

"I'd tie your hands behind your back to be sure you don't, but it would be so much more fun to punish you when I catch you. I know you won't be able to watch us and not stroke that sweet pussy of yours. Now spread your legs so I can see you."

Mary did as she was instructed. She threw her legs over the arms of her chair so she was fully exposed.

"Nice. Very nice. Don't you agree, Jean?"

"I do," Jean said. "She's so pink and juicy."

Mary looked Jean up and down. She licked her pouty lips. Jean felt a trickle run down her leg. Her arousal was apparent to all of them. She felt no shame, though. They were clearly all there to have a good time.

Dorothy took Jean's hand and led her to the bed. She lay on top of her, kissing her hard on her mouth. Jean was frantic in her need, her need to have Dorothy and be had by her. She rolled Dorothy over onto her back and pinned her arms above her head. She brought a knee up and pressed it into her center.

Dorothy ground into Jean's knee as the evidence of her arousal ran down Jean's shin.

Jean kissed down Dorothy's cheek to her earlobe. She sucked on it as Dorothy whimpered. She nibbled down her neck, stopping to pay close attention where it met her shoulder.

Jean released her grip on Dorothy to free up her own hands to run the length of her. Dorothy's body was shapely, with curves Jean couldn't ignore. She ran her hands all over her, reverently skimming over her soft belly, down a little, then back up to her voluptuous breasts.

She lowered her mouth and took one of Dorothy's nipples in it. She sucked on it voraciously, as if her life depended on it. First one, and then the other, she suckled long and hard. Dorothy moaned as Jean went crazy on her. They both heard the chair creak at the same time. They looked over and saw Mary with her hand between her legs.

"Stop that," Dorothy called. She quickly pushed Jean off her and stood.

She pulled Mary to a standing position. Jean watched from the bed, panting and frustrated from the interruptions. Still, she was fascinated as she watched the scene play out.

Dorothy spun Mary around and bent her over the bed. She delivered several sharp smacks to her rear end. Mary cried out, but Jean found herself oddly aroused at the display. Dorothy jerked Mary to make her stand again. She walked her back over to the chairs. Mary made to sit down.

"Oh, no, you don't." Dorothy said.

She walked over to a trunk and took out some sort of shackling device. Jean had never seen anything like it. She watched as Dorothy cuffed Mary's feet on either end of a long bar.

"You'll stand here and watch. And do *not* touch yourself."

Dorothy joined Jean on the bed again, and they went back to kissing, while Jean slid her hand between Dorothy's legs. She found her slick and ready. Jean longed to kiss her there, to suck on her lips and clit, but she had to have her at that moment, and this was the easiest way to do it.

Jean delved her fingers inside Dorothy, who raised up to meet her.

"Oh, my God, you feel amazing," Jean said. "You're so tight and hot."

"Fuck me, Jean. Fuck me like you mean it."

Jean thrust harder, each time plunging her fingers deeper inside Dorothy. She reached in as far as she could, then pulled them out, separating them as she did. Dorothy placed her own hand on her clit. She rubbed furiously as Jean continued moving in and out until Dorothy screamed, a guttural emission that shook the windows.

She collapsed on top of Jean, who lay breathing heavily from her exertion and the climax she reached when Dorothy came.

Dorothy rolled over and saw Mary standing there with her hands tangled in her hair. Her legs were wet from her juices.

"Were you a good girl?" Dorothy asked.

Mary merely nodded.

"Oh, Mary, what's the matter? The cat got your tongue?"

The pain was evident in Mary's eyes. Jean understood. Hyperarousal was one of the most painful states to experience. Jean wanted to bury herself between Mary's legs, to taste all the fluids that poured out of her. But she lay quietly on the bed while Dorothy unshackled Mary.

"Get Jean off," Dorothy said. "Make it quick."

Jean wanted to protest, to confess that she'd already come, but she didn't want to argue with Dorothy any more than Mary did. She lay back on the bed and let Mary climb between her legs again. Mary's talented tongue was more than Jean could stand. She felt her whole world quake as she came to a quick and powerful orgasm.

Jean flipped Mary on her back and climbed between her legs. She no longer cared about rules. Mary had the sweetest looking pussy and Jean had to taste her. She lapped at all the wetness she found, only creating more in the process. Mary was indeed sweet and salty, a heady flavor Jean couldn't get enough of.

While she continued on Mary, she felt fingers penetrate her. She realized Dorothy was filling her up. Jean rocked back and forth, meeting Dorothy's rhythm even while she tried to focus on Mary.

Mary wrapped her legs around Jean's shoulders and played her fingers through her hair. Jean's head was spinning. There were so many sensations at one time. She didn't know where to focus. She felt Mary deserved to come, but Dorothy had her teetering on the brink once again.

Jean fought through the cloud that filled her brain and focused her attention on Mary. Mary finally climaxed, leaving Jean free to do the same. She closed around Dorothy's fingers, wondering if she'd broken them with the strength of the orgasm.

They all fell together on the bed, their breathing labored. Jean reached a hand between Dorothy's legs again while Mary suckled on one of Dorothy's taut nipples.

"That's not necessary," Dorothy said, but neither listened. Together, they brought her to another climax.

Jean was content as she lay with Mary in her arms and Dorothy wrapped around her.

Dorothy abruptly stood.

"You should go," she said.

Jean looked at her, confused.

"Now? I mean, can't we languish in the moment?"

"No need to. We've had our fun. You need to get dressed and get out."

The cold Dorothy was back. Gone was any sign of the woman Jean had just shared passionate moments with. With a sigh, she got out of bed and quickly dressed. She turned back to Dorothy, but there was no one there. Mary and Dorothy were gone.

Jean shook her head as she let herself out of their suite.

David knocked on Jean's door early the next morning. She forced herself out of bed and opened the door.

"Oh my, don't you look lovely this morning?" David said.

"I'm sorry. I overslept."

"Well, doll yourself up and let's get going. We've got a horseback ride to go on."

Jean took a quick shower and applied her makeup.

"Dare I ask what had you up so late last night?" David asked.

"I'd rather not talk about it."

"Oh, so no shenanigans?"

"Well, there were shenanigans, but they were very strange," Jean said.

"Strange? Oh, my curiosity is piqued. Do tell. And don't leave anything out."

"I'm not going to talk about it, David."

"Oh, come on. You tell me everything. Who's the lucky lady?"

"There were two of them, if you must know."

"Oh, kinky. I hope you were careful. You have your reputation to think of."

"We were careful. Now, can we just go ride horses so I can forget about last night?"

"Of course. We need to be at the stables in fifteen minutes, so we'd better get a move on."

They drove to the outskirts of town and easily found the stables. Many of the riders in their group were already on their horses. David and Jean soon joined them. As they walked their horses to the rest of the group, Jean noticed a woman with a beautiful figure sitting atop an Appaloosa. She urged her horse in that direction.

The woman turned when Jean was even with her.

"Hello, Jean," she said.

"Well, hello, Maggie. This is a pleasant surprise."

A whirr of clicks could be heard as dozens of cameras went off. Jean simply turned to them and smiled.

"Now you've done it," Maggie said.

"You worry far too much. It won't hurt you to be seen horseback riding with me. And David's right here, so it's not like we're on an outing unchaperoned. You need to relax."

Maggie clicked at her horse and moved it forward. Jean urged hers to catch up. David caught up with both of them.

"Where's the fire, you two? The guide will be here soon and we'll get started."

"Maggie," Jean said, "This is David Duvall. David, this is Maggie. Though you'll have heard of her as Margaret Cranston."

"I have heard of you," David said. "I understand there's quite a talent behind that beauty."

Maggie blushed.

"Thank you. And I'm so glad you've heard of me. I'm working very hard to become as famous as Miss Sanders someday."

"I'm sure it's only a matter of time," David said.

"Miss Cranston was concerned about the press taking a picture of us together. You know how Hollywood can be. Any reason for a scandal. I was simply assuring her it was fine. Besides, you were in the picture with us."

"I'm sure you've nothing to fear, Miss Cranston. The press loves Jean, and being seen with her will only increase your exposure. I assure you it's not scandalous to be seen with her."

The guide came to the front of the group and led them out on the trail. Jean alternated between listening to the guide and focusing on the luscious body of Maggie in front of her. The ride was three hours and after, everyone was tired and thirsty.

"Where are you staying?" David asked Maggie after they'd dismounted.

"I'm at La Mirage."

"Join us at the pool. We'll have drinks," he said.

Maggie looked at Jean, who was holding her breath waiting for her answer.

"I'd like that," Maggie said.

"May we offer you a ride to the hotel?" David said.

"Yes, please."

They drove back to the hotel with pleasant banter, mostly between David and Maggie. Jean was too excited to talk much. She was hoping this afternoon would give her a chance to get to know Maggie better yet. She really liked her. She just needed to prove to her she could trust her not to get her into trouble with the press or anyone else.

They climbed out of the car.

"So, everyone get their suits on and we'll meet at the pool in fifteen?" David said.

Jean and Maggie agreed. They rode the elevator together while David walked over to talk to some people in the lobby.

"I'm very happy you've agreed to spend more time with me," Jean said.

"It's easier with Mr. Duvall around."

"But tell me you enjoy spending time with me, as well," Jean said.

"I do. Surely you must know that."

"I wonder."

"Well, you shouldn't. I do. I'm just afraid."

"Don't be. I've told you. I have to be careful. I'm not about to endanger my career so you've got to know if you're with me, I won't be endangering yours either."

They arrived at Jean's suite. She said good-bye with the promise of seeing Maggie in a few minutes. She was all smiles as she stripped out of her riding clothes and put on her swimsuit. Things seemed to be looking up.

She got to the pool before either David or Maggie. Maggie showed up shortly after.

"Where's Mr. Duvall?"

"He must have gotten held up. He'll be here soon, I'm sure."

As if on cue, David walked over carrying three glasses of champagne.

"I trust you ladies are as thirsty as I am."

"Thank you, Mr. Duvall," Maggie said.

"Please call me David."

"Thank you, David."

They sipped their champagne, then Jean stood.

"I'm going in. Who's with me?"

"I'll join you," Maggie said.

They walked down the steps and into the cool water. Jean felt her nipples harden and turned to see that Maggie's had done the same. She liked what she saw.

"This water feels amazing, don't you think?" Jean said.

"It really does. I feel it washing the dust of the trail off."

"I love a good swim."

She took off and swam the length of the pool and came back to find Maggie sitting on the steps.

"Are you not much of a swimmer?" Jean said.

"I was enjoying watching you."

"And?"

"I said I enjoyed it. You've got amazing legs, Jean."

"Thank you. I happen to enjoy all aspects of your body."

"How do you do it?" Maggie said.

"Do what?"

"Live as freely as you do and never get caught?"

"I'm very discreet, Maggie. And it's not like I'm with a different woman every night."

"You seem like the type."

Jean laughed.

"So you've said. I don't know where you get that idea."

"I don't know, honestly. It's just a feeling I get."

"Well, you need to let that feeling go. I like you. I really like you and want to spend more time with you."

"I'd like that, too, but as I've said, I'm scared. My career is just starting. I can't have it torpedoed with a scandal."

"And my career is at its high point. I'm not going to take any chances. I've told you that repeatedly. Besides, even David told you it would be good for you to be seen with me."

"But how many times would I need to be seen with you before rumors started?"

"We can face that when the time comes," Jean said.

They swam over to the bar and ordered more champagne. They sat in the water and sipped it.

"So, what does your evening look like?" Jean asked.

David swam up just at that moment.

"That's a great question. Tell us you'll join us for dinner."

"I'd love that. I really have no plans tonight."

"Wonderful. We'll meet at six o'clock in the dining room. I have standing reservations this week."

"It must be so wonderful to be part of Hollywood's elite. I can't imagine the way people must treat you, like royalty I'd imagine."

"It has its perks," David said. "But it doesn't come without sacrifices."

"Like privacy," Jean said. "That's the big one for me."

"Privacy to be sure," David agreed.

"How do you do it?" Maggie asked. "Live in a fishbowl?"

"Very carefully," David said. "You make a point of giving the press what they want. They love to see Miss Sanders here out on the town with actors, so we make that happen. Did you see the *Gazette* the other day? Pictures of Jean and Arthur Langdon were all through it. That's what the press wants, so that's what we give them."

"But what if they caught her in a compromising position?" Maggie asked. "What then? How would she recover?"

"There's the hard part," Jean put in. "There is no option to be caught in a compromising position. I must keep my nose clean at all times."

"But—" Maggie said.

"It comes with being a star," David said. "You'll understand soon enough. For now, though, it will only do you well to be seen with Jean. It'll get you press time. That's important."

"Okay. If you say so."

"I do. Now you two need to get out of the sun. And it's time to get ready for dinner. I'll see you in the lobby at six."

They dried off and Jean and Maggie once again found themselves alone in an elevator.

Jean reached out and took Maggie's hand. She didn't resist.

"Say you'll come to my room tonight," Jean said. "Make me the happiest woman in the world."

"Let's just see how dinner goes," Maggie said.

"Come on. Today's been magical. Surely you've felt it."

"I have, Jean. I'd be lying if I said otherwise. But let's see how dinner goes with the press presence and all. If they're about to follow you upstairs, I'm not going to chance it."

"Fair enough," Jean said, though she noticed Maggie was still holding her hand.

At six o'clock, Jean arrived in the lobby to find Maggie and David already there. They stood as she approached and Jean couldn't take her eyes off Maggie. The light pink dress she wore had a daringly divulging décolletage. Jean enjoyed the view very much.

David was the first to speak.

"Jean, my dear, you look radiant as always." He kissed each of her cheeks. "That blue satin is perfect for your sapphire eyes. And you got a little color today, which also sets off your eyes and that perfect blond hair of yours."

Jean flushed profusely.

"Thank you, David. I must say, you look quite dapper as well. That white dinner jacket looks wonderful with the plum accoutrements."

David bowed.

"But," Jean continued. "I do believe it's our lovely Miss Cranston who takes the cake tonight."

"She does look delightful," David said.

"Thank you both. I feel like a little girl playing dress up." Maggie said.

"Nonsense," Jean said. "You are anything but a little girl."

She felt David's gaze boring into her and chose not to acknowledge it. If David hadn't figured it out before, he certainly had at that moment. She would be discreet and David needn't worry.

"Jean?" David said. "A word with you, please?"

"Oh, David, not now. Really. Don't be a party pooper."

They walked to the dining room with David between them. He kept glancing at Jean who kept her head held high and smiled as the flashes went off all around her. They arrived at their table and the press was right behind them. They continued taking pictures.

"Are you officially mentoring Miss Cranston?" someone called out.

David stood and faced the crowd.

"Right now, all we're doing is having dinner. Please allow us some privacy."

The mob backed away and David sat back down.

"They're vultures," he said.

"But what if they decide something else about Miss Sanders and myself?" There, she had said it.

"Miss Sanders is America's Sweetheart. She's as straight as a board. You'll never read anything to the contrary because there's no way they'd ever see anything else. Am I right, Jean?"

"Yes. You're exactly right," Jean said.

"Now, what would you two like as appetizers?"

Dinner was ordered and David got down to business.

"I'm thinking tomorrow night you should dine with Spencer Roberts," David said to Jean. "He's the new kid on the block, but everyone is saying he's got what it takes to make it big. It might do you both well to be seen together."

"That sounds good," Jean said.

"I've seen some of his movies," Maggie said. "He's quite good."

"So, dinner and dancing with him tomorrow. I'll set it up."

"I'm glad our calendar was free for tonight." Jean looked at Maggie.

"So am I," Maggie said.

David leaned forward and lowered his voice.

"You two better be careful."

"You know we will, David. I'm America's Sweetheart, not a dyke."

"Good. You know damned well, you're my cover as much as I'm yours much of the time. If you're questioned, I'll be questioned. And that simply will not do."

"Relax. It will all be fine."

"I'm as scared as you are, David," Maggie said. "That's why I was afraid to come to dinner, afraid to even talk to Jean on the trail. But she's assured me she's careful and so have you."

"But now I see the way you two look at each other. Jesus help us if this gets out."

"It won't," Jean said adamantly.

Arthur Langdon was coming into the dining room as they were leaving. Jean threw her arms around him and allowed him to kiss each of her cheeks. They turned to the cameras and smiled.

"It was good seeing you. Enjoy your dinner," Jean said.

"Thanks. I was wondering if we might get together again?"

"I think I'm free the night after tomorrow."

"Great, so dinner and dancing?"

"Sure," Jean said. "I'll meet you here at seven."

"Sounds great."

"See you then."

Jean acted like she ignored all the cameras, but she was very aware of her expression and her proximity to Arthur in every shot. She was adept at making herself seem like the person the country thought she was.

They left the dining room and made their way to the bar where they each had a brandy. The soft warm liquid soothed Jean and made her mellow. It also made her wish she was alone with Maggie. She saw the amber liquid on her lips and longed to lick it off.

"Well, I think I'm going to turn in," Jean said.

"Please be careful, you two," David said.

"I'll leave then you two leave together. No one will be any wiser," Jean said.

"Sounds easy enough," Maggie said.

"I hope it will be."

"May I have a bottle of brandy to take to my room?" Jean asked the bartender. She signed the receipt and left the bar.

She had slipped out of her dress and into a robe when she heard a knock on the door.

"It's open," she called.

In walked Maggie, looking as timid as a virgin.

Jean stood and crossed the room to her. She pulled her in for a hug.

"Please relax."

"I'm scared, Jean."

"Did anyone see you come up here?"

"No. That's not what I'm scared of. I'm scared I'm going to fall for you. Hard. And you'll just up and leave me behind."

"That's not going to happen," Jean said. She caressed Maggie's soft cheek. "I give you my word. I'm not going anywhere."

"I wish I could believe you."

"Let me prove it. For now, let's just enjoy tonight."

Jean poured them each a glass of brandy. She handed one to Maggie, who drank from it gratefully. Jean saw the brandy on her lips and bent to taste them. The kiss was soft and tender, not as powerful as the kiss Jean knew she would give her soon.

"You should get out of that dress," Jean said.

"I suppose I should," Maggie said.

"I'd love to help you," Jean said.

Maggie turned her back and Jean unzipped her dress. She carefully slid it off her shoulders and hung it in the closet.

"No sense you leaving here in a wrinkled dress."

Jean watched as Maggie unhooked her bra and her breasts fell free.

"You're beautiful," Jean said.

"I'm glad you think so," Maggie said.

"I do."

Jean pulled Maggie to her and kissed her again. She lost herself in the kiss. Her head was swimming as their tongues met. She pulled Maggie closer and held her tight.

When the kiss ended, Jean was dizzy with need. She rested her forehead on Maggie's.

"That was something else," Maggie said.

"Yes, it was. There's a slight flavor of brandy on your lips. It just makes you warmer to kiss."

"Is that why you brought a bottle to your room?"

"One of the reasons. You'll see what I have in store."

Maggie sat on the bed and took off her underwear and stockings. Soon she was sitting there nude for Jean to appreciate.

Jean dropped her robe and laid Maggie back on the bed. She climbed on top of her. The heat of their flesh meeting drove Jean into a frenzy. She kissed Maggie's lips, her eyelids, her ears, and her neck. She was feverish with need.

"Wait here just a minute," Jean said.

Maggie looked confused, but she propped herself up on her elbows to watch Jean.

Jean came back with her glass of brandy. She trickled a little over each of Maggie's breasts.

"How does that feel?" she asked.

"It feels chilly," Maggie said.

"But it's going to taste warm."

Jean licked one of Maggie's breasts like a lollipop. She swirled her tongue all over it, licking up the brandy. She closed her mouth on Maggie's nipple and sucked hard.

"Oh God, yes. That's it," Maggie said.

Jean moved to the next breast and did the same. There was no brandy left on Maggie when she was through.

"Oh God, Jean. Please, I can't take much more."

Jean took her glass and poured a trail of it down Maggie's belly and between her legs. She licked along the trail, lapping up the brandy and feeling Maggie's gooseflesh as she went.

When she got between her legs, she reverently stared at Maggie for a moment.

"I want to draw this out. I want this to be perfect," she said.

"It will be," Maggie said. "Please, I can't wait much longer."

Jean lowered her mouth and licked the length of Maggie. The brandy combined with her natural flavors to give her a musky taste that Jean couldn't get enough of. She buried her face as she went about her business, licking and sucking every inch between Maggie's legs.

Maggie pressed Jean's face into her as she raised off the bed and cried Jean's name as she reached her first orgasm.

Jean smiled against Maggie's clit, happy to have provided her such pleasure. She moved her fingers inside Maggie, who screamed almost immediately as the next waves of pleasure coursed over her.

Maggie pulled Jean up to her and kissed her hard, tasting her own orgasm on her lips. She had to have Jean just as desperately as she'd needed Jean to have her.

She rolled over on top of her and kissed down to Jean's pert nipple. She drew it into her mouth and rolled her tongue over the tip. Jean tangled her fingers in Maggie's hair.

She slid a hand down Jean's soft belly until she found her swollen nerve center. She rubbed it gently before slipping her fingers inside.

Jean arched her hips and Maggie plunged deep inside her. Jean writhed on the bed, needing release, so close to release. Her nipple was in direct communication with her clit, so Maggie's suckling had her on the brink. Now feeling her fingers pounding inside took her close. So very close. But she didn't come. Why couldn't she come? She was so close.

Maggie moved her fingers back to Jean's slick clit, and that's all it took for Jean to feel the powerful orgasms crash over her again and again. She lost count of how many times she'd come.

When she could finally open her eyes, she saw Maggie's looking down at her.

"You're something else," Maggie said.

"So are you," Jean said.

They kissed then curled into each other's arms. Jean held Maggie close while they fell asleep.

❖

Jean woke the next morning to an empty bed. It took her only a moment for the events of the previous evening to come back to her. She sat up and looked around the room. There was no sign of Maggie. The only hint she'd even been there was her half empty glass of brandy.

Jean climbed out of bed and went to the closet. Maggie's dress was gone. She moved to the desk and sat down, head in hands. It was then she saw the note.

"I woke up in the middle of the night and decided it would be safer to leave then. I had a wonderful time. I really like you, Jean. My room number is 1218. Please call me today.
All the best,
Maggie"

That made Jean smile. She liked her. She really liked her. Because Jean had fallen hard for Maggie the minute she'd met her. She couldn't explain it, but she had. And then, the dinner when they'd talked about Maggie's father just sealed it. Jean wanted to protect Maggie. And that's what she intended to do.

Jean showered and rang David's room.

"Hello?" David said.

"Meet me for breakfast?"

"More like brunch. Are you just waking up?"

"I am. So, brunch. Meet me in a half hour?"

"I'll be there."

She hung up and picked up the receiver again. She wanted to call Maggie with every bone in her body. But she might still be asleep and she didn't want to wake her. She showered and dressed and went down to the dining room.

David already had a table. Jean joined him.

"I'm famished."

"So am I," a voice from behind her said.

She turned to see Maggie standing there.

"Maggie! I didn't think you'd be awake yet."

"I just woke up."

"Won't you join us?" David asked.

"Thank you, but I'm already eating with people. I'm trying to rub elbows while I'm here. I'm sure you understand."

Jean hoped her disappointment wasn't apparent on her face.

"I don't blame you. Palm Springs is the place to see and be seen," she said. "Good luck."

"Thanks," Maggie said, then lingered.

"I'll call you later," Jean whispered.

"Thanks," Maggie said again. "I look forward to it."

David watched the exchange.

"Tell me it's nothing serious," he said.

"I can't, David. I've never felt this way before."

"Oh, sweet Jesus. Listen, Jean…"

"Don't you worry. We'll keep it under lock and key. You need to trust me."

"Oh, that reminds me. You're on for dinner with Spencer Roberts tonight."

"Wonderful. And Arthur Langdon tomorrow night. That should keep the vultures at bay."

"It should, but it won't necessarily. Not if you do something stupid."

"I won't. David, please. This is getting so droll."

"I see the way you two look at each other. It's just a matter of time before someone else does, too."

"Fine. I'll talk to her about that. Okay?"

"You'd better make sure she understands, Jean."

"I will. Now, can we eat?"

Brunch was over and Jean pleaded tired to get out of tennis with David. She needed to take a nap to be ready for drinks and dinner and a late night. As soon as she got to her room, she dialed Maggie's room.

"Hello?" Maggie said.

"Hi," Jean said. She sat on her bed and twirled the phone cord around her finger.

"How was brunch?" Maggie asked.

"It was good. What are you doing right now?"

"I'm not sure. I might go down to the tennis club or I might go to the baths. I should probably do something like that."

"Why don't you come to my room?"

"Are you serious?"

"Yes. I miss you."

"I'm on my way."

As soon as the door closed behind Maggie, she was in Jean's arms. They kissed like two people who hadn't seen each other in years; the previous night's heat simply a precursor for the morning's.

They fell onto the bed, limbs tangling and lips locked.

Jean's hand slid up Maggie's skirt to find her panties slick with her want. Jean pushed them to the side and slipped her fingers in. She found the soft spot just inside that she knew drove Maggie crazy.

Maggie wrapped her legs around Jean and pumped against her, as she cried out her release.

Jean rolled off Maggie.

"Thank you for coming by."

"I needed that."

"I need you," Jean said.

Maggie lay back on the bed.

"What's going on, Jean? I'm confused."

"Why are you confused?"

"There's this feeling I get around you. I'm giddy and happy, and when I'm not around you, all I think about is you and when I might see you again."

"That's good. Don't you see? We have something special," Jean said.

"But I barely know you."

"We're getting to know each other. It's the beginning of something big."

"We're not allowed something big. Don't you realize that?"

"I fail to believe that," Jean said. "I believe if we want it bad enough, we can make it happen."

Maggie pulled Jean to her and kissed her.

"So, what does your day look like?" she asked Jean.

"I don't know. I have dinner with Spencer Roberts tonight. That's the only thing I have on my agenda. What about you?"

"I don't have a thing until four. Then I have drinks with Jason Fredericks."

"The director?"

"One and the same."

"Good for you."

"Thanks," Maggie said.

"We should go to the pool," Jean suggested.

"That would be wonderful."

"Meet me there."

Jean kissed Maggie and quickly changed to her swimsuit.

Chapter Five

Jean called David to let him know she and Maggie were going to the pool. She invited him to come along. He said he'd join them and Jean felt a sense of relief. She understood Maggie's trepidation. Regardless of the brave front she attempted to put up, she was scared they'd be found out. Yet she couldn't stop herself. She had to spend more time with Maggie.

All three arrived at the pool at the same time. David sat on a lounge while Jean and Maggie took a dip. They swam to the bar.

"So, tell me about you," Maggie said. "Tell me about your childhood and stuff."

"There's not much not known about me. My life's pretty much an open book."

"Tell me anyway." Maggie looked at Jean with adoration in her eyes.

"You mustn't look at me that way, sweetheart," Jean whispered.

"What way?"

"The way you just did. Not in public anyway. That kind of look shows up in pictures."

"I'm sorry. It's just so hard."

"I know."

"So, anyway, about your childhood."

"I grew up in a small farm town in Kansas."

"Brothers and sisters?"

"No. I'm an only child."

"Are you close to your parents?"

"I am. They are very supportive and proud of all I've become," Jean said.

"That must be wonderful."

"It is."

"So what's your biggest regret, Jean?"

"That I can't be completely open about my relationship with you."

David popped out of the water between them just as the cameras went off.

"Ah, now I look like quite the lady's man," David said. "I've got a lovely on either side of me."

Jean laughed, but Maggie looked terrified.

"It was perfect timing," Jean said.

"But it might have been bad," Maggie said.

"Just remember how you look at each other and you'll be safe," David said. "Right?"

"Right," Jean said.

"I hate to break up the party, but, Jean, you and I must get ready for drinks and then you have dinner with Spencer."

"Is it that time already?"

"It is. Maggie? You'll excuse us?"

"Will I see you later?" Maggie whispered.

"Tonight. Say eleven? In my room?" Jean said.

"I'll be there."

Jean and David were enjoying cocktails when up walked Dorothy Martin and Mary.

"Hello, you two," Jean said.

"Hello," Dorothy said. "We've been looking all over for you."

"You have? I've been pretty visible this week. You know, giving the people what they want."

"What we want," Dorothy said, "is to have drinks with you after dinner tonight. Are you available?"

Jean thought of the fun she'd had with them before and felt herself grow wet at the idea of another round. Still, she had Maggie now.

"I can't tonight. But thank you so much for thinking of me."

"Your loss," Dorothy said as she walked away.

"Drinks with your dream girl and you said no?" David whispered in Jean's ear.

"That was the other night," Jean said. "This is a new night. I have plans already."

"You've got it bad."

"That I do."

"Well, hello, you two," a voice boomed from behind them. "May I buy you a drink?"

They turned to find Spencer Roberts, all six foot three inches of him leaning over them. Jean noticed he seemed more focused on David than herself.

"That would be wonderful," David said.

Jean swore he almost swooned. She wondered if David would be joining them for dinner, but then thought maybe dinner with her was as big a cover for Spencer as it was for her.

He returned with their drinks and they found a table.

"It's sure nice to finally meet you," he said to Jean. "You're a legend. I can't believe you agreed to dinner with me tonight."

"You're quite the rising star, Spencer. It's a pleasure to have dinner with you. By the way, this is David Duvall, the director."

"I'm a big fan," Spencer said. He shook David's hand a little longer than necessary.

Jean smiled to herself as she sipped her champagne. It seemed that the evening might be fun and entertaining after all. At least Spencer wouldn't be as fresh as Arthur had been.

The men spent most of the next hour visiting, and Jean was left to survey the bar scene. She was almost bored when she saw Maggie walk in. She looked stunning in her cocktail dress. Jean felt her heart soar. Maggie looked over at her and smiled, then turned her attention to the bar.

Before she could order a drink, Arthur Langdon was at her side. He bought her a drink and steered her out of sight. Jean was disconcerted but hoped Maggie would be able to hold her own with the likes of Arthur. At least she was being seen with America's heartthrob, which would do her a world of good. Before turning back to her table, Jean saw the flashes go off in Maggie's direction. Jean smiled. Things were working out well.

She turned back to hear David say, "We'd love that, wouldn't we, Jean?"

"I'm sorry. I couldn't hear. What would we love?"

"Spencer has invited us to play doubles tennis tomorrow with Dorothy Martin."

Wow, Jean had wanted her for so long and now she just wasn't going to go away, was she?

"That sounds wonderful," Jean said.

"Do you know Dorothy?" Spencer asked.

"I do. Are you close?"

"We've been in a couple of movies together. She seems like a nice enough dame."

"She is," Jean said.

"Well," Spencer stood. "I see that it's time for us to relocate to the dining room."

He put out his elbow for Jean to take. As soon as she did, cameras went off all around them.

"David, it was very nice to meet you and I'll see you on the courts tomorrow morning."

"Enjoy your evening," David said.

Spencer and Jean entered the dining room, where they were greeted with more flashes and stares from some of the patrons.

"Do you ever get used to it?" Spencer asked.

"Not exactly. Sometimes you wish you didn't live in the limelight."

"I've already figured that much out."

"But you do get used to cameras and the press any time you go out in public. Even if you wish they weren't there."

"I'm not used to it yet. I feel like they should be going after movie stars, not me."

Jean laughed.

"Oh, Spencer. You are indeed becoming quite the movie star."

"It just hasn't set in yet, I guess."

Jean found Spencer to be a charming young man. She enjoyed her dinner with him and gladly accepted his invitation to go dancing after.

"I must say, though, I'll have to retire early if I'm to play tennis in the morning," Jean said.

"Fair enough." Spencer laughed. "I agree to those terms."

They danced around the room for what seemed like hours before Spencer let Jean plead exhaustion.

"I had a wonderful time tonight, Jean. I do hope we'll be working together soon."

"I hope so, too," Jean said.

She kissed him on the cheek as cameras clicked, then hurried toward the elevators.

She had no idea what time it was, as it was considered impolite to wear a watch to these kinds of events. You never want to get caught checking the time when dining or dancing with a handsome leading man.

Jean arrived at her room. She checked the time. She had twenty minutes before Maggie got there. She filled the bath with warm water and poured in salts the hotel provided. It was pure heaven. She felt any strains melt away and only thoughts of Maggie were in her mind as she dried off.

There was a knock at the door at precisely eleven. Jean opened it slightly and peeked her head around.

"Hello, Maggie. Please, come in."

She stood back, naked, and held the door open for her.

"Don't you look nice?" Maggie said.

"Thanks." Jean laughed. "I just stepped out of the tub. Let me grab a robe."

"No need. I like you like that. I'll step out of my clothes and then we'll be even."

Maggie stripped and hung her clothes in the closet. She lay next to Jean on the bed.

Jean propped herself up on one elbow and looked down at Maggie.

"So, I saw you had drinks with Arthur Langdon. I'm so sorry. The man is a letch."

"He really is. He does not like to take no for an answer."
Jean was concerned.

"He didn't force himself on you, did he?"

"He finally got the message with a well placed knee in the elevator. I hated to do it, but he left me no choice. Then I got off on the wrong floor and walked up the stairs to mine, so he won't know what floor I'm on."

She shuddered.

"I'm sorry." Jean stroked Maggie's arm.

"It's okay. I'm safe with you now."

"And no one saw you come to my suite?"

"Not a soul. The reporters seem fairly content to stay in public areas."

"That they do. Which I appreciate very much. I like being given some semblance of privacy."

"And what do you plan to do with said privacy tonight?" Maggie said.

Jean lowered her mouth to capture Maggie's. She kissed her sweetly as she skimmed her hand the length of her body.

"I plan to enjoy it in so many ways," she said.

"Mm. I like the sound of that."

"I thought you might."

She kissed Maggie again, softly at first and then with more passion as the fire in her raged.

"I can't explain what you do to me, Maggie. You make me crazy."

"I hope this is a good thing?"

"It's a very good thing."

They kissed again, a long, drawn out series of kisses, some hard and some soft, sometimes simply lips meeting and sometimes tongues dancing.

"God, I want you," Jean said.

"I'm here for you."

"But I want to take it slow. I want you to know what I feel for you. This is so much more than just sex, Maggie."

Maggie gently eased Jean off her.

"Is it? Are you sure?"

"I've never been more sure of anything."

"What is it, though? And why me?"

"I don't know the answers to those questions, Maggie. I just know in my heart of hearts that you're the one for me. I've never felt this way before. Tell me you feel it, too."

"I do, Jean. I do and it scares me."

"No reason to be scared. Never be scared of me."

Jean kissed her again while she dragged her hand up to a full breast. She kneaded the soft, supple skin before closing her finger and thumb around her hard nipple.

Maggie gasped and Jean twisted the nipple while she sucked and nibbled Maggie's neck. Maggie's breathing got faster and faster and Jean continued what she was doing, pushing Maggie, daring her not to come.

Maggie mewled softly as she reached her orgasm. When her breathing returned to normal, Jean let go of her nipple and moved her hand down between Maggie's legs. She slipped it past Maggie's swollen clit and went inside her. She stroked her slowly but steadily, playing her like a fine instrument until she cried out.

"You like that, huh?" Jean said.

"God, yes."

Jean allowed her fingers to play over Maggie's clit, pressing it into her pubis, rubbing circles around and around.

Maggie spread her legs wider as she gyrated against Jean. It took no time at all for the orgasm to hit and she screamed Jean's name.

Maggie rolled over on top of Jean and kissed her. She kissed her slowly, languidly. Jean ran her fingers through her hair as Maggie kissed slowly down to her breast. She took a nipple in her mouth and drew the tip of her breast in with it. She sucked hard, lightly brushing Jean's breast with her teeth.

Jean felt Maggie's tongue playing with the tip of her nipple and shuddered. She was wet and throbbing and craving more. She was a quivering mess by the time Maggie placed her hand between her legs. Maggie stroked her determinedly, knowing just how to touch her to make her crazy.

And crazy Jean was. She was frantic, so close to the edge.

"More, baby. Give me more, Maggie. I need to come."

"How's this?" Maggie slid another finger inside.

"Oh God, yes. Oh God, yes. That's it!" Jean felt the ball of heat form in her very core. She felt it pulsing, ready to break lose. One stroke, then another, and then the heat coursed through her veins to her extremities. The orgasms cascaded over her like waves on the shore.

When she came to her senses, Maggie was still inside her.

"Oh my God, baby. That was amazing," Jean said.

Maggie slipped her fingers out and massaged Jean's clit for just a second before Jean cried out again.

"No more," Jean said. "I can't take any more."

They snuggled together.

"Will you be here when I wake up in the morning?" Jean said.

"I don't think so. It's best that I sneak out in the middle of the night."

"But there's never any press up here on our floors."

"Still, that's not a chance I'm willing to take. For now, please just hold me while I sleep."

❖

Jean woke the next morning to an empty bed, as promised. Still, this time wasn't as bad because she'd been expecting it. Still, her arms felt empty. She wondered how Maggie could slip out of bed and leave so soundlessly. Jean wished Maggie would at least wake her up to say good-bye.

She got out of bed and showered, then went down to the lobby to meet David for tennis. He showed up, all smiles.

"Good morning, Jean."

"Good morning. You're in a good mood this morning."

"I'm looking forward to some more time with Spencer. You can't blame me."

"And how much time did you have with Spencer last night?"

"Oh, Jean, you know I don't kiss and tell."

"I know quite the opposite." Jean laughed.

"And come on, you know you're excited about playing with Dorothy Martin."

"I would have been excited before Maggie. Now it'll be a pleasant diversion. Nothing more."

"Well, hello." Dorothy greeted Maggie with a kiss on the cheek. "It's good to see you again."

"It's wonderful to see you, too."

Jean looked over to see David and Spencer with bright smiles on their faces. She couldn't help but be happy for

David. It had been a long time since he'd been this happy. She just hoped he'd remember all his admonishments to her to be careful.

"Let's get this game underway," Spencer said.

The game was fun, with the teams not quite evenly matched. Spencer clearly had much to learn in the game. But they enjoyed themselves and treated themselves to drinks after the match.

"So what does your evening look like?" Dorothy asked Jean.

"Dinner and dancing with Arthur Langdon."

"And after? Mary and I would love for you to join us again."

"I can't tonight. Thank you."

"Did you not enjoy yourself?" Dorothy lowered her voice.

"I did." Jean was honest. "But I can't join you tonight. I'm sorry."

She wished she could tell them she was seeing someone, but even they couldn't be trusted. She would do nothing to jeopardize her relationship with Maggie.

After a few drinks, Jean excused herself.

"Where are you going?" David asked.

"To the pool. I need to cool off."

"We'll join you." Spencer stood. David stood next to him.

"That would be great," Jean said. "Will you be joining us, Dorothy?"

"I'm sorry. I'll have to beg off this time. Will you meet Mary and me for drinks later?"

"Sure. That sounds swell. I'll have time before I meet Arthur."

As soon as Jean was in her room, she dialed Maggie's. No answer. Jean really wanted to see her, but understood that

Maggie had people to mingle with. Still, she was disappointed. She fought the disappointment and quickly donned her swimsuit.

When she got to the pool, Spencer and David were already there, looking chummy. Cameras clicked. Jean went over and stood between them, all smiles. More cameras went off as she seemingly flirted with one and then the other of them.

"You two better take it easy when in public," she said.

"We're just a couple of gents having drinks by the pool," David said.

"And the cameras seem to love that."

"The cameras didn't care until you came out here," Spencer said.

"Not true. I'm not here to argue. I'm just asking David to be careful. Just as he always asks me to be careful."

She glanced around the pool area to see who was there. She saw the mystery woman from earlier in the week. Had it really only been a few days ago? It seemed like forever, like Maggie had been the only girl for her ever.

She swam some laps then swam up to the bar. Arthur Langdon was there.

"Hello, Jean," he said. "Are we still on for dinner tonight?"

"We are."

"I look forward to it. We had such fun last time."

Jean fought to keep the smile on her face.

"And we'll have fun this time," Jean lied.

CHAPTER SIX

Jean met Dorothy and Mary at the bar. Dorothy looked decidedly uncomfortable in her cocktail dress, but Mary looked delicious in hers. They both smiled when Jean walked up. Dorothy stood.

"Thank you for meeting us," Dorothy said. "I'm sorry you won't be able to meet us later."

"Me, too. But I've got plans tonight."

"You have plans every night now. You're really using this vacation as a publicity opportunity, aren't you?"

"Guilty," Jean said.

"Wouldn't you rather take some time for yourself? Like you did the other night?"

"Look, Dorothy," Jean said. "That was a lot of fun. But I have to be careful. As do you. We can't take chances like that very often."

"I don't take chances. I'm sure you would be discreet as you were the other night. Otherwise, I wouldn't ask you."

"Let's just enjoy our drinks," Jean said. "What are you working on, Dorothy?"

"When vacation is over, I start a new movie. It's about a woman in the workforce during the war. I think it'll be a hit."

"Congratulations."

"I'm sure you'll have many roles lined up when you get back."

"We'll see."

They drank and laughed and Jean was amazed that she wasn't drawn to either woman. Somehow, her desire for Dorothy had dissipated, and she was sure it had nothing to do with the night they'd spent playing. She was really serious about Maggie. And now she knew just how much.

When six o'clock arrived, Jean excused herself and met Arthur Langdon for dinner.

❖

Dinner was pleasant. Arthur seemed to be less drunk than their previous dinner and thus much better behaved. Jean was never uncomfortable. She actually enjoyed herself. He was charming and interesting, full of anecdotes about movies he'd worked on and people he'd worked with.

After dinner, Jean excused herself and went to her room. She called Maggie's room, but again got no answer. Sad and lonely, Jean got ready for bed.

She was awakened by a knock on her door.

"Who's there?" she called.

"It's me. Maggie."

Jean opened the door and pulled Maggie into an embrace.

"I missed you today," Jean said.

"I missed you, too."

"Where were you?"

"I was out with some producers and directors most of the day. Trying to push myself. I met with your studio heads, too. I'm hoping they'll sign me."

"That would be wonderful," Jean said.

"I'm sorry I woke you up."

"No. It's great. I'm happy you're here."

"Would you mind just holding me? I really just need to feel your arms around me," Maggie said.

"Sure. That'd be swell." Jean calmed her racing libido. Holding Maggie would be heaven. If Maggie wasn't in the mood for sex, that was okay. At least she'd come to see her.

Maggie lay down and Jean spooned in behind her. Maggie felt wonderful in Jean's arms. Jean felt like they were both just where they were supposed to be.

Jean awoke the next morning to find Maggie sleeping soundly next to her. She was delighted that Maggie hadn't snuck out during the night. She gazed at her longingly as she ran her hand over her body. Maggie stirred, but didn't wake.

Jean took a nipple between her fingers and gave it a gentle tug. Maggie murmured in her sleep. Jean knew she should let her sleep, but she looked too beautiful and inviting lying there. She had to have her.

She bent over and sucked on the nipple nearest her. She felt it harden in her mouth.

"Oh," Maggie said. "Good morning to me."

"Mm hm."

Maggie took Jean's hand and placed it between her legs.

"I need you, Jean."

Jean moaned when she felt how wet Maggie was.

"I need you, too."

Jean took Maggie with slow, sensuous movements. She took her time, studying every inch of her and giving her the attention she needed. When Maggie finally climaxed, Jean was throbbing with her own need.

Maggie was quick to return the favor. Though anything but slow, Maggie hurriedly, passionately loved Jean until she cried out as she came.

They lay together catching their breaths.

"So, what now?" Maggie asked.

"What do you mean?"

"It's back to reality. Back to real life. The one where the reporters are at your doorstep every minute of every day," Maggie said. "Where does that leave us?"

"If you're asking if we'll still see each other, the answer is yes."

"But how?"

Jean was silent for a moment.

"Move in with me."

"Are you crazy?"

"Maybe. A little. But why not? We can say it's temporary while I mentor you. It'll be good press for both of us."

"I don't know, Jean. I have a place."

"Which is costing you rent, right? Move in with me and you won't have to pay rent."

"I'm not sure about this."

"Look, I love you and don't want to miss any time with you."

"You what?"

Jean realized what she'd said. Her heart stopped. She had no idea how Maggie would respond.

"I said I love you. Tell me you love me, too."

"Oh, Jean! I do. I do love you, too."

"Then tell me you'll move into my house. There's plenty of room. You've seen it."

"I have. And there is. But I'll only need to be wherever you are. That's all I want. All I'll ever want."

"Oh, Maggie. You've made me so happy."

They made love again and were relaxing in each other's arms when a knock on the door startled them.

"Jean? Are you in there?" David called.

Jean quickly donned a robe while Maggie hid in the bathroom. Jean opened the door.

"Good morning, David," Jean said.

"It smells like sex in here," David said.

"Good to see you, too. What can I do for you?"

"You can get ready for breakfast. We're running late. We need to get on the road."

"Can Maggie join us for breakfast?"

"Are you sure she hasn't left yet?"

"I'm fairly certain."

David arched an eyebrow at her.

"Yes, I suppose you are. Very well. She can join us. But please hurry."

She closed the door and Maggie came out of the bathroom. She quickly dressed and kissed Jean.

"I'll meet you downstairs in just a minute."

Jean walked with a spring in her step as she entered the dining room. She felt lighter than air as she crossed to where David was sitting.

"That must have been some night," David said.

"Why, I'm sure I don't know what you're talking about." Jean laughed.

Maggie walked up and draped a hand over Jean's shoulder as she walked by.

She sat across from Jean and greeted David.

"Hello. So, are you all set to head back to Hollywood?"

"I am," David said. "Although I'm not so sure Jean is."

"I will be. Give me a half an hour after breakfast and I'll be all set."

Spencer walked up then.

"So, today it's back to reality, huh?" he said.

"So it is," David said.

"Well, don't lose my number when you get back, please."

"I won't." David smiled. "I'm keeping it safe."

"Wonderful. Well, enjoy your breakfast."

They watched as he walked off.

"Maggie's going to be moving in with me," Jean said.

David choked on his eggs.

"Excuse me?"

"Yes. I'm going to officially mentor her. She'll live with me full-time. I'll teach her everything I know."

"Is this wise?" David said.

"We've thought it all out," Jean said. "It's foolproof."

"The press is going to go crazy with this."

"I think Jean and I have thought this out very carefully," Maggie said. "There's no reason for anyone to be suspicious. It gives me a reason to be there all the time and it makes her look even more loveable. It's the perfect idea."

"I'm not comfortable with this, but I certainly can't stop you."

Breakfast was over and Jean hurried up and packed her bags. She followed the bellboy to the lobby where she met David. The drive home was quiet. Jean was lost in her recollections of the past week, most prominently those of Maggie. She was beside herself with excitement at the thought of Maggie moving in.

"Have you seriously thought about this business of moving Maggie in with you?" David seemed to read her thoughts.

"I have. I think it will be wonderful."

"How long have you known her, Jean?"

"Not long, but she's the one, David. I can feel it in my bones."

"You forget, in Hollywood, she can't be 'the one.' Eventually, you'll need to find a man and assume a fake marriage."

"And if I end up doing that, she can still live with us."

"Tongues will wag, Jean."

"Speaking of wagging tongues, what's up with you and Spencer?"

"Isn't he a hunk?"

"I suppose." Jean laughed. "He's not really my type."

"Oh, Jean. He's the cat's meow."

"I'm glad you've found someone, David. I'm really happy for you."

"Thanks. Although it'll be hard to see him in Hollywood. The press is all over him."

"I'm sure they are."

"And I'm not about to move in with him," David said.

"Lesbians are different," Jean said. "It doesn't take us more than a couple of dates to know if she's the one. And trust me, Maggie is the one."

"I'm just asking you to think long-term. It wouldn't do for America's Sweetheart to be a spinster. You're going to have to find a nice man to marry. Spencer, for example."

"He'd be the perfect cover, to be sure, but I'm not going to give up my time with Maggie."

"Suit yourself. But I do think you and Spencer should start being seen together."

"I think you're right about that. If he'd be willing to do that."

"I'll speak to him."

❖

The following day, Maggie began moving into Jean's house. The press was out in full force and Jean finally stepped out front to address them.

"I'm sure none of you is a stranger to Miss Margaret Cranston's name. She is moving up the ranks of Hollywood's finest actresses. I have decided to take her under my wing and mentor her. I'll be working with her on readings as well as showing her the ropes. She'll have the south wing of my home during this process. Does anyone have any questions?"

"Was this approved through your studio head?" one young man said.

"I've yet to speak to him about this. I'm sure there'll be no problem."

"How does David Duvall feel about this? Aren't you two an item?" another reporter asked.

Jean smiled.

"David and I are merely friends, darling. He thinks it's a wonderful idea."

The questioning quickly changed.

"Who is your current romantic interest, Miss Sanders?"

"I think this interview is over," Jean said.

"But you had dinner in Palm Springs with a couple of Hollywood's leading men. Didn't sparks fly?"

"You'll have to pay attention to see who I end up with. Now, if you'll excuse me."

She turned and walked back to her house.

"How did it go?" Maggie asked.

"Not bad. I think they'll accept this as a logical situation. Though it will mean I'll have to date more. As will you, I presume."

"Ah, the charades we must keep up."

"It's the life we live."

"Yes, it is."

Jean took Maggie in her arms.

"I'm so glad you're here, Maggie."

"I'm glad to be here."

Jean kissed her softly, then more passionately.

"I need you," Jean said. "Let's go to my room."

"I've got so much more unpacking to do."

"It will wait."

They were interrupted when Betty walked in.

"Miss Sanders? May I ask what's going on?"

"Betty. Hello. You did a fine job keeping up the house while I was away. May I introduce you to Margaret Cranston? She'll be staying with us indefinitely."

"Miss Cranston," Betty said. "It's a pleasure to meet you. I feel like I've met you before."

"Miss Cranston is an actress. I'm sure you've seen her in a movie."

"Oh, that's wonderful," Betty said. "Welcome."

There was an awkward moment of silence. Jean didn't know what to say. She wanted to be sure Betty understood there'd be no more playtime between them, but she didn't want to say anything in front of Maggie. She finally cleared her throat.

"Miss Cranston and I will be in my room going over some lines. Please see that we're not disturbed."

"Yes, ma'am," Betty said.

Jean stopped at the foot of the staircase and allowed Maggie to go first. She enjoyed the sway of her trim hips as they climbed the stairs ahead of her. She couldn't wait to get Maggie undressed.

As soon as the door was closed, Jean was at work removing Maggie's clothes. She tossed them carelessly on the couch until Maggie stood naked in front of her.

"Oh, yes," Jean said. "So very nice."

She pulled Maggie to her and kissed her hard on her mouth. Her tongue darted into Maggie's mouth, and Jean fought to keep her balance as her head swam. She quickly stripped out of her own clothes and pulled Maggie onto the bed with her.

Maggie's flesh was hot as it pressed into Jean. It seared her everywhere their skin met, leaving her mark, making sure Jean knew she'd been there. Jean rolled over and pulled Maggie on top of her, running her hands up and down her back, down to her shapely ass. She cupped and squeezed the glorious mounds and spread her cheeks slightly. She ran her finger down Maggie's crack but stopped before she found her taboo entrance.

Maggie writhed on top of Jean, pressing her wetness all over. She rubbed it over her torso before grinding into her leg. She kissed one of Jean's breasts. She sucked on the supple white flesh long enough to know she was leaving a mark, but she didn't care. Jean's skin was so soft and tasted so good. Maggie moved to another area and sucked there as well.

"You're driving me crazy," Jean said.

"I want to make you scream."

"Keep doing what you're doing and you will."

"What do you like, sweetheart? Tell me your favorite things."

"You're my favorite thing. I like anything you do to me," Jean said.

"Well, that leaves it wide open, doesn't it?"

"No pun intended?"

Maggie laughed.

"None at all."

She kissed down Jean's body. She stopped to spend time at Jean's adorable belly button. Maggie didn't know why, but she found it impossible to resist. When she was through there, she moved lower and kissed Jean's inner thighs. Again, she left marks on her thighs, confident no one would see them but the two of them.

"Oh, doll," Jean cried. "Do you ever know how to make me feel good."

"Mm," Maggie said as she licked up the tender skin. When she came to where Jean's legs met, she paused briefly.

Jean was tense, ready for release. All she needed was a touch, a lick, a caress and she knew she'd come unglued. She felt Maggie's tongue on her and she pressed her head to her. She gyrated her hips as she ground her pussy into Maggie's mouth.

Maggie was moving her tongue voraciously all over Jean and it was almost immediate when the tension reached its zenith, then everything broke loose as Jean was lost in her orgasm.

She returned to reality clutched in Maggie's arms.

"Oh, wow. That was really something else," she said.

"I love how powerful your orgasms are," Maggie said.

"Only with you are they like that. I mean, don't get me wrong. I always enjoy my orgasms, but only you take me to that level, doll."

"Well, I'm glad I can do that for you."

"You do. It's amazing. How experienced are you, Maggie?"

"What kind of question is that? You don't want to know the answer do you? I mean, all that matters is you and me, right? Nothing before counts, does it?"

"I suppose you're right," Jean said. "I was just curious. I'm sorry I asked."

"You're forgiven."

Jean kissed Maggie as she ran her hand over her body.

"I love your body."

"It loves you."

"Mm." Jean kissed her harder as she found her center with her fingers. She stroked her slowly at first, then faster as Maggie moved against her. She slid her fingers out and moved them to Maggie's clit, which felt hard enough to explode. She spun careful circles on it until Maggie clenched her to her and held on as she came.

"I say we nap for a while," Jean said.

"Wonderful though that sounds, I really need to unpack and get settled in."

"Very well. Let's get dressed."

❖

They went back downstairs and Maggie headed to her boxes while Jean went to the kitchen for something to eat. She ran into Betty.

"She's very pretty," Betty said.

"I suppose she is."

"Is she your lover?"

"You know better than to ask me questions like that."

"Will I still be your lover?" Betty said.

"I think we should stop that. I don't think it was healthy."

"Maybe not healthy, ma'am, but it sure was fun."

"Yes, Betty, it was. But I need to be free now."

"To enjoy your new toy," Betty said.

"She's not a toy."

"If you insist."

"I do, and if I hear you refer to her that way again, you'll be out of a job."

"Yes, ma'am."

CHAPTER SEVEN

The months passed, and Jean had never been happier. Maggie had been signed to her studio, so they occasionally saw each other on the lot. But it was the nights that made everything right in Jean's world. It wasn't simply the lovemaking, though that was certainly the best she'd ever had. There was so much more. Little things like dining together or enjoying a glass of wine in the garden. Everything she did with Maggie made her happy.

Maggie was becoming a force to be reckoned with in the film industry. She had signed on to play supporting actress in one of Hollywood's newest movies. Spencer was the leading man, so Jean had high hopes for the film.

Jean had signed on to play the wife of yet another war hero. She was the star of the movie, with Arthur Langdon the leading man. Even with Arthur's insatiable ego, there was no doubt who was taking center stage. Especially with David as the director.

As they'd expected, Jean and Maggie had to go on occasional "dates" with men to keep up the charade that they were interested in them, but those dates came fewer and further between as their relationship blossomed.

One day at work, the head of Jean's studio called her in to his office.

"Yes, sir?" she asked as she sat down.

He threw a copy of *The Wag* on the desk. *The Wag* was the gossip rag in Hollywood. The reporters were always looking for scandals in Hollywood. They were the ones camped out at her doorstep and the ones taking pictures in Palm Springs. She'd just seen some the night before at dinner with David.

"What's this?" She picked it up.

Jean Sanders and Margaret Cranston in Love Nest? was the headline.

"Where did they get this?" Jean said. Her insides were trembling. She was terrified. They had to do damage control.

"Is it true she lives with you?"

"Yes," Jean said. "I'm trying to help her out."

"She can't afford to live on her own?"

"Not that kind of helping her out. You know, I'm mentoring her. Coaching her."

"The studio has coaches for that. You don't need to do that."

"It just seemed like a nice thing to do."

"So you are living with her and you didn't think the press would have a field day with that?"

Jean picked up the paper and looked at the cover photo. It was a picture of Maggie and her enjoying a cup of coffee out by the pool. She supposed the feelings between them was apparent. Damn it.

"Sir, you know I'm not that way. I date some of Hollywood's leading men. Surely you don't believe this nonsense."

"I don't want to," he said. "But the public eats this stuff up. I want her moved out of your place as soon as possible. And I mean that. Or you will both be suspended."

Jean finished filming that day and hurried home. She hoped no one had shown Maggie a copy of the paper. She walked in to find Maggie in tears. She went to her, but Maggie simply beat on her chest.

"This is all your fault," she said.

Jean moved away and held Maggie by the shoulders.

"It's all gossip, doll. It's what these papers print."

"But it's true, Jean. It's all true." Maggie sobbed. "It's not just some made up story."

"But readers don't know that. We'll simply make a statement about it."

"It's too late. We're ruined."

"It's never too late," Jean said. "But I do think you should move out."

"So you ruin my life and then kick me out?"

"What else can we do? We need to play it close to the vest for a while. Soon another scandal will come up that will have tongues wagging. For now, we say I've coached you as much as I can. You're taking off on your own. And you're moving out."

"How long will it take before I find my own place? How long until we can prove they're wrong?"

"I say we start looking immediately. Look, Maggie. The studio head is the one who told me about it. He's saying you move out or I'm suspended. We don't want this tainting either of our careers."

"I'm sure it already has," Maggie said. "Just when I was really starting to make it, too. Why did I listen to you? You promised me we'd be safe."

"Look, we go to the papers, we categorically deny everything. We simply say that yes, we were having coffee one morning. Where's the sin in that? We then announce that since people with corrupt minds have twisted this into something perverted, you'll go ahead and move out. We can do this, Maggie."

"And then it's over."

"What?" Jean was stunned. "What do you mean?"

"I mean it's over, Jean. I won't jeopardize my career any further."

Jean felt her stomach muscles tighten. She fought tears.

"Maggie, I love you. I thought you loved me."

"I did. I do. I don't know. But I can't keep seeing you."

"You're overreacting. I get it. You're in shock. But once we get it all straightened out, you'll see. We can keep seeing each other. We just need to be careful."

"That's what you said about me moving in here," Maggie said. "And we were careful, or so I thought. And look where that got us."

"We'll date more. With men. We'll find safe men and be sure to be seen with them more often."

"That's what we've been doing, Jean. And it hasn't worked. Clearly."

Jean ran her fingers through her hair.

"Shit, Maggie. Please don't do this. At least allow me to buy you lunch in the cafeteria sometimes. Or we can sneak somewhere in the middle of the night sometime."

"That's not going to work. They'll follow us. You know it. No one is going to let either of us out of their sight until the story has blown over. As for the cafeteria, I suppose two women eating lunch together wouldn't cause a stir. But we can't do it for a while."

"I'll go crazy without you, Maggie. You've got to know that."

"We don't have a choice."

Deflated, Jean slumped into a chair.

"Now, if you'll excuse me," Maggie said, "I've some packing to do."

She walked off just as the phone rang. Betty came into the room.

"Ma'am, Mr. Duvall is on the phone."

"Thank you. I'll take it."

"Hello, David."

"Jean, dear. I just saw. I'm so sorry."

"Did you just call to say you told me so? Because I'm in no mood."

"No. I called because I truly am sorry. I wanted you two to be happy. I wanted to know someone like us could make a go of it. How did they get that picture anyway? It was clearly a private moment."

"Who knows? They're sneaky asses. They could have easily been hiding in our garden."

"I'm really sorry. Will you go to dinner with me tonight?"

"I'd love that. I need to get out of here."

"I'll send a car."

"Thanks. I'll see you in a little while."

She walked into the kitchen where she found Betty about to start dinner.

"You can go home now, Betty. I'll be having dinner with David tonight."

"What about Miss Cranston?" Betty said. "Will she be dining out as well?"

"She's no longer our concern. She's moving out."

"She's what? Why?"

"It's of no concern to you," Jean said.
"Yes, ma'am."

❖

Dinner was nice, nothing special. Very few pictures were taken of them. She was furious. She wanted to know how anyone found out about her and Maggie's morning coffee together. It was their time.

"Well, I hope she's moving out," David said.

"Yes. Mr. Goldsmith gave me an ultimatum."

"Really?"

"Whatever happened to the good old days when no one took *The Wag* seriously?"

"I think it's that Thomas O'Leary who's got everyone paranoid."

"What can he possibly do?"

"He wants to run us out of town," David said. "He thinks homosexuals and communists should be thrown into jail."

"Well, I've done nothing wrong and shouldn't be threatened with suspension just because I fell in love."

"It's not that you fell in love, Jean. It's who you fell in love with. And you know that."

"It's still not fair."

"I know."

"How's Spencer?" Jean asked.

"He's well. Scared, but well."

Their conversation was interrupted when Arthur Langdon walked up.

"Sorry about the article in *The Wag*," he said.

"Thanks. It was just garbage."

"I'm sure it was. Let's prove them wrong. Have dinner with me tomorrow night?"

"I'd love to," Jean lied.

"Great. I'll send a car for you at seven."

"I'll be ready."

"Good to see you both."

They watched him walk off and sat in silence for a few moments.

"I'm sorry you have to go out with him."

"Him of all people," Jean said. "He's so weird. And doesn't like to take no for an answer."

"I remember. I hope you'll be okay."

"I'm sure I will."

"Let's go get a few drinks," David said when they'd finished dinner. "I think we both deserve that today."

"Okay, but I can't have too many. My director will have my head if I'm not on my game tomorrow." She laughed.

"I'm sure your director will be as understanding as he can be."

"I appreciate that, David. Have I told you lately how much your friendship means to me?"

"I appreciate that, Jean. Yours is important to me, as well."

Jean came home to an empty house after dinner and drinks. She climbed the stairs to her bedroom with a void in her heart. Her world was empty without Maggie. She hoped they'd be able to continue to see each other, but she knew everyone was right. It would be too detrimental to her career.

❖

The following morning, Jean cursed her empty bed. She threw her arm over her face and was tempted not to go in for the day's shooting. She couldn't do that, she knew. They were already behind schedule.

She forced herself out of bed. She donned a robe and made her way to the kitchen. She found a plate of bacon and eggs and a cup of hot coffee. Betty was washing dishes.

Jean tried to eat but felt nauseous. She sipped some coffee out of necessity.

"Will Miss Cranston be back to move more things today?" Betty asked.

"I suppose so."

"I'll have to clean her rooms very well when she's all out."

"I suppose so," Jean repeated.

"You're not much in the mood to talk this morning, are you?" Betty said.

"Not particularly."

"And you've hardly touched your breakfast. Eat up. You'll need your energy."

Jean knew she was right, so she ate a piece of bacon. It tasted like cardboard to her.

"I'm sorry, Betty. Nothing tastes right."

"I cooked them just the way you like them."

"Oh, I'm sure you did. It's me. I just don't feel like eating."

"Well, you have to, so make yourself eat an egg, at least."

Jean obliged and fought to keep the egg down. Nothing was right in her world. Just the day before, Jean and Maggie had had breakfast together, neither of them even slightly suspecting how the day would end. But it had ended. And it had ended badly. Now a piece of Jean's heart was missing and she knew she'd never get it back.

She finished her coffee and Betty poured her another cup.

"Are you going to be able to work today?" Betty asked.

"Of course. I have a job to do, people who count on me. I have to work."

"You just seem so out of sorts."

Was Betty really that naive? Had she not seen that Jean and Maggie were lovers? Jean didn't have the energy to spend contemplating that. She remembered when Maggie had moved in, she'd told Betty no more sex. Surely Betty had figured things out then?

Jean finally left the table and got ready for work. She made it to the studio with moments to spare.

"I'm glad you made it," David said quietly.

"Of course. I'm a professional."

"Thank you."

Arthur walked across the stage to Jean and David.

"Are we still on for dinner tonight?"

"Of course."

"Great. Shall we get to work?"

"Yes," David said. "Go get your makeup on and get out here."

Jean went to her dressing room where her makeup artist went to work on her.

"You've got some dark circles under those eyes today, Miss Sanders. Do I need to remind you how important sleep is to you?"

"I know," Jean said. "I just had a hard time sleeping last night."

"I'm sure. It's the scandal, isn't it?"

Did the woman have no sense of decency?

"I'd rather not talk about it."

"Well, of course, we all know it's not true. But still, it's got to be hard to be on the front page with such horrid accusations."

"It's certainly not easy."

"I'm sorry you're in that position. You shouldn't have to defend who you are. I mean, you did such a wonderful thing, taking Miss Cranston in to coach her and help her out and this is how you're repaid? Sinful, if you ask me."

Thankfully, her makeup session ended and she got dressed in costume. She was out on the stage before Arthur.

"Are you ready for this?" David said.

"I am. I'll be happy to have something to take my mind off things for a while."

"Excellent. Because we do need to be spot-on today. We need to make up time."

"I get that, David. And I'll do my best. I do believe I'm ready."

Arthur walked out of his dressing room.

"Places," David shouted.

❖

The day went well, with Arthur making more mistakes than Jean. It made Jean feel good and it didn't hurt their schedule. They still made up time.

"Great job today," David said. "You were both excellent. Arthur, be a little better prepared on Monday, though, okay?"

"It wasn't my fault. I couldn't hear my cues."

Of course it wasn't his fault, Jean thought. He did nothing wrong. She was fine with her cues. She spoke loudly and clearly. He just missed them. But he wouldn't admit that. God, he exhausted her. And to think she had to go out to dinner with him in a few hours. The thought turned her stomach anew.

"You're both released for the weekend. Have fun."

"Thanks, David," Jean said.

She drove home, filled with dread at the forthcoming evening. She should have told him that she'd changed her mind, but she didn't so now she'd have to spend a few dreadful hours with him.

Jean dressed quickly, with little care given to how she looked. She made sure she would look good for pictures, but didn't go overboard so Arthur would think she had dressed up for him. She was ready when the car arrived at seven.

She was taken to The Pearl, a fancy restaurant on Sunset Strip. She knew this was an opportunity she'd have to take advantage of. The press were outside the door, as well as teeming inside.

The lights flashed as soon as she stepped out of the car.

She heard people calling her name, but ignored them.

"Miss Sanders! Miss Sanders!"

She fought through the crowd of reporters.

"Miss Sanders," someone called. "Miss Cranston is here, too. Are you meeting her?"

The question made Jean stop in her track. Maggie was there? Her heart skipped a beat. Maybe they'd have a moment to speak. She had butterflies in her stomach. She felt like a teenager with a crush. But she couldn't help it. She was hoping to see Maggie.

She finally got herself together and turned to walk into the restaurant. Arthur already had a table. He stood and kissed her cheek when she walked up.

"You look beautiful, Jean."

"Thank you. You look quite dapper."

He was wearing a gray sports coat with black slacks and a white shirt.

"You're too kind," he said.

When she picked up her menu, he took it from her.

"No need to waste your time. I'll order for you."

"I am fine ordering for myself."

"Yes, but I know the restaurant. I know what's good. I'll order for you."

Jean fumed internally. She wanted to rip her menu from his hands, but didn't want to make a scene. Instead she glanced around the crowded venue, hoping to catch a glimpse of Maggie. There were too many people there. She couldn't see her.

"You know," Arthur was saying. "I think you and I should date more often."

"What? Why?"

"I really like you, Jean. And I know you like me. I mean, what woman in America wouldn't want to date me?"

"But, Arthur, it would be so awkward on movies where we costar. Like now. Things could be awkward on the set tomorrow."

"No, it wouldn't. I would still be the lead. You'd still be just under me. Nothing would change. We're both adults, after all."

Jean fought hard to control herself. She felt her face flush in anger.

"Now you're blushing," he said. "You can't hide your feelings from me."

"If you'll excuse me," she said. "I need to powder my nose."

She walked to the ladies' room and took several deep breaths. She dabbed at her eyes to keep the tears from falling. She leaned her face against the cool wall.

"Jean?"

She turned.

"Maggie!"

They hugged quickly before Maggie pulled away.

"What are you doing here?"

"I'm having dinner with Arthur."

"Why do you look like you just lost your best friend?"

"Maybe because I have," Jean said.

"I understand. Well, look, I'm going to get out of here before anyone sees us. Take care, Jean."

Jean leaned against the wall, fighting the waves of nausea.

Jean took several more deep breaths and made her way back to her table. Arthur was looking as smug as ever and she fought the urge to slap him.

"I've already ordered," he said. "So, what shall we do tomorrow night? I think a trip to the theater would be nice. We'd certainly make a splashing sight, don't you agree?"

Jean nodded. She sat in a stunned silence, unable to make a sound.

"You know, Jean. It would do you good to have a steady beau. Especially after yesterday's *Wag*."

"I know," Jean managed. "That was so uncalled for."

"You'd better hope Senator O'Leary doesn't catch wind of it. You may never act again."

"I think you credit that man with more power than he actually has."

"Oh, I don't think so."

"I feel like he's on some sort of private witch-hunt," Jean said.

"He wants to clean up our industry. I have to admire the man."

"There's nothing wrong with our industry."

"If you don't count the commies and the homos. I have a feeling he's really going to get rid of them all. Maybe not today or tomorrow, but someday soon, he'll rock our Hollywood."

"Or maybe he'll just leave well enough alone."

"He'll clean up Hollywood and he'll clean up our government. He won't stop until we're running cleanly. I really admire the man."

Jean had nothing further to say. Their dinner arrived and she was tempted to say she was allergic to the snapper. But it was delicious and she ate every bite.

"Thank you. That was very good."

"I told you. I know what you'd like. I see no reason to let a woman order her own food."

"You let me in Palm Springs."

"That's a different environment. More lax. You'll not look at a menu while we're dating."

After dinner, Jean claimed exhaustion. Arthur walked her to her car. She expected him to open the door to let her in, but instead, he pressed her into the car and kissed her hard on her mouth. She tried to turn her head away, but he held it in place.

"Arthur, please," she said when the kiss ended.

"No need to beg," he said and leaned into her as he kissed her again.

She felt his manhood swell and press against her. She managed to break the kiss.

"I should go," she said.

He took her hand and placed it on his swollen member through his slacks.

"Surely you won't leave me like this," he said.

"I don't think a lady should be spoken to like that," Jean said.

"Maybe you really are a dyke."

"I'm no such thing."

"Well, don't expect to get off so easily tomorrow night. I'll send a car for you at six so we can have dinner before the theater."

"I don't know," she said.

"I do. I'll see you tomorrow night."

Jean called David first thing the following morning. She told him about her date.

"I don't want to see him again," she said.

"I don't blame you. But I think it's important right now."

"I won't sleep with him, David. I can't."

"I don't blame you there, either. You just need to make that clear."

"I tried last night. He called me a dyke."

"Just be a lady," David said. "He'll have to respect you."

"I do have a reputation to worry about," Jean said. "I can't go from being labeled a lesbian one minute to being a slut the next."

"Very true. Be firm with him, Jean."

"I will. Thanks for listening to me."

"You're welcome. I know you'd do the same for me."

"I would indeed."

Jean spent the rest of the day lounging around the pool. The warm sun and cool water made her feel much better. Her mind wouldn't rest, but physically she felt healthier.

Until it was time to get ready for her date. Then the nausea started again and she had to fight to keep her stomach down. She dressed in a long, white gown with diamonds in her ears and around her neck. She looked stunning and knew it. The cameras would love her. Unfortunately, so would Arthur. But it was the theater so she had to dress up.

The car arrived at precisely six o'clock and she helped herself to a drink when it started on its journey. She sipped her bourbon until they arrived at The Monte Cristo, one of the higher end restaurants in Hollywood. She knew he was serious about her by taking her there. She chastised herself to relax and enjoy her evening and not to worry about the end of the night until it got there. Although she was nauseous when he sent her car home.

She knew she wouldn't be able to keep up the charade too long. It would be different if it was a man she didn't despise. However, it was good for her to be seen, so she needed to be strong, at least for a little while.

Dinner was a repeat of the previous night. She sat seething while Arthur ordered for her. She held her tongue as he chastised her that women had too many rights nowadays, that they needed to be more subservient like they used to be.

"I long for the good old days. Things used to be right in the world."

"I don't see what's wrong with the way things are now," Jean said.

"Of course you don't. You're too strong-willed, Jean Sanders. That's why it's so good that we'll be dating. I'll teach you how to stay in your place."

"Arthur, I'm sure I disagree with that. I know my place. Millions of Americans know my place. It's front and center."

"Sure, when you're acting. But in real life, you need a strong man to stand behind and care for his every need."

"Are you saying you can't take care of yourself?" she said.

"Of course I can. I just shouldn't have to. That's why we have women."

"And I think if a man has to rely on a woman for everything, he's a very weak man."

"You really do need to be taken down a few notches," Arthur said.

Jean's stomach was in knots by the time dinner arrived. She didn't think she'd be able to eat, but the filet Arthur had ordered was cooked to perfection and tasted too good not to enjoy.

After dinner, they took his car to the theater. Flashes went off all around them. People called to them to look over so they could take their picture. She knew they made a striking couple.

"Are you two an item now?" one person called.

Jean was about to respond when she heard Arthur.

"What do you think?"

"But what about Margaret Cranston?"

"What about her?" Arthur said before steering Jean inside. She wanted to cry. She wished she were with Maggie right then. She missed her so much.

Finally, the curtain went up and she was able to lose herself in *Joan of Lorraine*. The performance was stunning, and she found herself caught up in the characters on the stage. She felt everything they felt and was left raw at the end of the show.

She was brought back to the present as the lights went up. She saw Arthur stand out of the corner of her eye and felt his hand at her arm. She stood and allowed him to escort her out.

The cool evening air felt good. She took a deep breath.

"Steeling yourself for what's to come?" Arthur smiled.

"What? No. I'm enjoying the fresh air. That theater was so stuffy."

"It was. And boring as hell."

"I thought it was incredibly moving."

"I don't like plays. I mean I'll go to be seen and all, but I think it's a waste of time. Especially a play about women."

"You chose it," Jean said. "What would you rather be doing?"

"Spending time alone with my woman."

Jean felt the knot return to her stomach. She fought tears. She had to make the most of the situation. She felt like she was doing penance for her time spent with Maggie.

Their car arrived and Arthur opened her door for her. He presented himself as such a gentleman in public. Little did they know.

As soon as they were in the car, he pulled her to him and kissed her hard on the mouth. She fought as hard as she could, but he was too strong. His grip was tight and she knew she wasn't going to win the struggle. She fought back gags as his tongue explored her mouth.

He pushed her onto her back and climbed on top of her. His hand moved all over her body.

"Stop," she said.

"You know you want this," he said.

"No. I don't."

"Sure you do."

He closed his hand over her breast. His breathing was labored and she could feel his excitement against her leg.

"No," she said sternly. She closed her hand around his wrist and tried to pull it away. He was too strong.

He was bruising her breast.

"You're hurting me. Please."

"It feels good and you know it."

He was grinding into her leg. She wanted to knee him with everything in her power. She tried to move her knee up, but he had her pinned down. She couldn't move.

He roughly kissed down her neck. She felt his whiskers chafing against her soft skin. She was in pain all over.

"Please," she said. "Please stop. Arthur..."

She tried to slap him, but he caught her arm.

"Don't you dare," he said.

The car stopped and Jean breathed a sigh of relief. She knew she was going to get out. But Arthur didn't move. Instead he moved his hand to her back and began unzipping her dress.

"No!" she screamed.

"Don't fight it, doll. You know you want it."

"No. I don't. We're at my house and I'm getting out."

"Invite me in."

"No."

"Then we'll take care of things out here." He finished unzipping her dress. The feeling of his fingers on her skin made her nauseous. She gagged. She tried to fight it, but couldn't.

"What the hell?" Arthur said. "What the hell is wrong with you?"

"Nothing. I told you I didn't want you touching me."

"You better get a grip. I'll touch you whenever I want. And you'll let me. And you won't fucking gag. Now invite me in."

"No. I won't. And I won't be seeing you anymore. Now get off me."

Arthur climbed off her.

"There's something wrong with you. Any woman in America would want me."

"There's nothing wrong with me. There's something wrong with you, forcing yourself on me like that."

"You know what I think? I think you're really a lesbian and that's just sick."

"I'm not." Jean couldn't believe she'd said the words so easily.

"Yes, you are. You like women. That's not right. You're not right. You need help."

"I don't. I'm fine. I don't need help. I just don't like to be forced."

"Get out of my car, you fucking dyke."

Jean fought to keep her dress on as she hurried into her house. She heard the car speed off before she got to the front door. What a gentleman, she thought.

She went upstairs and undressed. She climbed into bed and pulled a pillow close. Why was life so unfair? All she wanted was Maggie. She was easy to love and loved her back. And she was gone. Jean wondered if all men were going to be like Arthur. If that was the case, she would abstain from dating. No, she knew she couldn't do that. She would have to be seen with men, but she wouldn't let anyone pressure her into anything steady unless she really liked them. Not that she would ever love them. But she would at least have to like them. And they'd have to be gentlemen. She wouldn't allow anyone to treat her the way Arthur had.

She thought again of Maggie and the love they'd shared. She cried, softly at first, then with gut-wrenching sobs. She finally cried herself into a restless sleep.

❖

Tensions were high on the set Monday morning. The day would be spent filming touching scenes between the main characters. Jean was spot on in her acting, but Arthur wasn't believable.

"What is your problem?" David said.

"Nothing. I'm doing a great job," Arthur said.

"No, you're not. You're stiff as a board here. I need you to make me believe William loves Ruth. You're acting like he doesn't want anything to do with her."

"It would be easier if my costar wasn't a dyke," Arthur said.

"You've had the same costar this whole time," David said. "She wasn't a dyke Friday and she's not a dyke today. I don't know what you're problem is, but we really don't have the option of getting further behind by having to reshoot a bunch of scenes today. Now get your shit together and act."

Jean fumed inside that Arthur would try to make his incompetent acting about her. She didn't think of him as Arthur when she was in role. He was William O'Brien to her, the love of her life. She didn't know why he couldn't put aside his differences and simply act.

It took several more takes but they finally got the scenes shot. When David called it a wrap, Jean hurried to her dressing room. She lit a cigarette before she even began taking off her makeup. She knew they still had another few weeks of filming to go and she wasn't looking forward to working with Arthur every day. At least they'd gotten most of the love scenes out of the way that day.

She took another long draw on her smoke. She set it in the ashtray and proceeded to take off her makeup. Next came her costume. She left it lying over the back of a chair as she dressed. Someone in costume would put it away. She sat in her underwear finishing her cigarette. It tasted good and did much to soothe her frayed nerves.

She finally put the cigarette out and dressed. There was a knock on the door.

"Who is it?"

"It's Virginia."

"Who?"

"I'm one of the stagehands. Mr. Duvall is requesting you to have dinner with him tonight."

"Tell him I'll be out in just a moment."

Jean smiled to herself. Dinner with David would be just what she needed. She would be able to relax and forget about her troubles for a few hours.

She left her dressing room and started toward David, but Arthur was talking to him. So she hung back and waited. Arthur finally walked off and Jean approached David.

"What was that about?" she asked.

"We'll talk about it at dinner. Are you ready?"

"I am."

"Let's go, then."

They chose a small, out of the way restaurant where Jean was able to relax without being in the scrutiny of the public's eye.

"I take it you didn't have the best weekend?" David said.

"Not even close. The man is an animal. He tried to take advantage of me in the backseat of his car Saturday night. I mean, he even got as far as unzipping my dress."

"Oh, Jean. I'm so sorry."

"It was horrible. I tried to fight him off, but he was too strong. I finally gagged which is what got him to stop."

"So that's what all the dyke talk was about today."

"Right. Apparently, any woman who doesn't want him in the back of a car is a dyke."

"I'm so sorry again. I'll find a nice man for you to date, Jean. I promise."

"Ugh. I wish it didn't have to be this way," Jean said. "I wish I could be with Maggie."

"But you can't."

"How are you and Spencer?"

"It's touch and go," David said. "We see each other when we can, but it's usually just a planned accidental meeting. We can't take chances either. Especially after what happened with you and Maggie."

"I'm hoping the pictures everyone got over the weekend will take the heat off me for a while."

"I hope so. I'm glad he took you to places where you could be seen. At least that will help."

"It better. Otherwise it will all have been for naught. I can't allow myself to believe that. I hope we make front page this week."

"Well, you're a very handsome couple."

"Someone asked if we were an item and he asked what they thought. That's got to be worth something."

"I'm sure it will be. Again, I'm sorry you went through all that, but it'll all be worth it to clear your name."

"I don't know, David. It still doesn't feel altogether worth it."

"Suspension from the studio? Losing your status as America's Sweetheart? Darling, not having that happen certainly makes it worth it."

"I suppose you're right."

"Goldsmith will see that picture and immediately forgive you. Trust me."

"Wouldn't that be wonderful?"

"It will, Jean. It really will."

❖

The rest of the week was tiresome for Jean. Arthur was an asshole and made shooting difficult at best. Jean did her best to ignore him. David spent a lot of time shooting scenes where the stars were with their supporting actors and actresses, which made it much easier to move ahead in filming.

She had just wrapped a scene Thursday afternoon when she was called, once again, to Mr. Goldsmith's office. She walked in.

"What can I do for you?" she asked.

"Explain this." He tossed *The Wag* onto his desk.

Jean picked it up. Her mouth dropped open. There was a picture of Maggie and herself in her pool. They were holding on to the edge, heads close together.

America's Sweetheart With Her Own Sweetheart the page read.

Jean sunk into her chair. She opened the magazine to page three to read the rest of the article. There were pictures of Arthur and her, but the article surmised he was a cover for her. She felt the tears forming and blinked them back. One escaped. She wiped it away.

"What did I tell you about this?" he said.

"She moved out. There never was anything between us. Surely you know that."

"And what about Arthur? Is he a cover?"

"We went on a couple of dates. That was all. It was nice," she lied.

"I won't have a scandal in this studio."

"Sir, there is no scandal. There never was. I don't know why they're still printing pictures. She lived with me. I told you that. Sure, we spent time in the pool. As friends. There's nothing more to it. You need to believe me."

"But you swear she moved out?" he said.

"I do. I promise."

"And another thing, there's a new movie coming onboard. I want you to be the star and her to be the supporting actress. I don't need bad publicity about that."

"Sir, we'll work well together. And we're always professional. Please believe me."

"Fine. I'll give you the benefit of the doubt this time. But if the bad press continues, that suspension can easily happen."

"Yes, sir."

CHAPTER EIGHT

David finally called the film a wrap three weeks later. They were a week behind schedule, so tempers flew toward the end. Jean did her best to maintain her professionalism, but it was hard working with someone like Arthur.

He finally got into his role, which was beneficial to filming, but he was such a prima donna that he would refuse to shoot his scenes unless the scenes before had been perfect. Even if David called them good. Which led to fights between David and Arthur and tension on the set.

Jean was glad the movie was a wrap. It was a pleasant autumn afternoon, and she walked off the set with a spring in her step. She had two weeks off before her next movie, the one that would costar Maggie. She was thankful that Spencer would be her leading man. She'd spent enough time with Arthur Langdon to last a lifetime.

She went home and found Betty cleaning the living room. She looked sexy as hell in her uniform. She was bent over dusting, and Jean could almost see the heaven between her legs. She coughed.

Betty stood and turned.

"I'm sorry, ma'am. I didn't hear you come in," she said.

"That's all right. You may proceed."

"Yes, ma'am."

Betty went back to dusting. Jean eased herself into a chair and watched.

"Ma'am?" Betty said. "Is something wrong?"

"Not a thing." Jean was enjoying the view. Betty had gorgeous gams, and the fishnet stockings really showed them off. As she watched, she noticed Betty's exaggerated movements. Clearly, she was trying to get a rise out of Jean. And it was working. Jean was tempted to walk over and run her hand up a thigh. She knew how creamy her skin would be and was fully aware that one touch would have Betty more than ready for her.

As she sat there, glued to her chair, she wondered what was stopping her. Betty wanted her. Obviously. So why not indulge herself? Why not indulge them both? Jean stood and started to cross the room. Out of the corner of her eye, she saw a statue that Maggie had given her. She picked it up.

Maggie. She was the only woman Jean wanted. She'd had enough meaningless encounters. Now Maggie was the only one that mattered. Even though Betty would no doubt make her feel better for the time being, it would only feel worse when it was over. Because Betty wasn't Maggie. No one was.

She turned and went upstairs to her room. She closed the door and lay on her bed, hugging her pillow tight to her chest. She just wanted to lock herself away until the new movie started.

The door opened and Betty walked in.

"Ma'am? Are you okay?"

Jean didn't look up.

"I'm fine."

"You don't seem fine. Why are you home so early?"

"We wrapped up shooting."

"You should be celebrating," Betty said.

"Maybe tonight. Not now though."

"Maybe we could have our own celebration now."

"Betty, I'm not in the mood."

Betty crossed to the bed and laid a hand on Jean's hip.

"I don't believe that, ma'am. You're always in the mood. When was the last time you had some attention?" Jean's body betrayed her. Even the light touch of Betty's hand sent her libido charging.

"It doesn't matter," she said.

"It should."

Betty climbed on the bed and lay behind Jean. She ran her hand over Jean's body.

"I'm ready for you any time, ma'am. All the time. Just say the word."

Jean rolled over and faced Betty. She saw the longing in her eyes. Betty leaned forward and kissed Jean's neck. Jean closed her eyes at the sensations flowing through her. She took Betty's face in her hands and kissed her. It was a hard, passionate kiss she felt throughout her body.

Betty sat up and started unbuttoning her uniform.

"Stop," Jean said. "No. I can't. This isn't right."

"What's not right? We've done this hundreds of times before."

"That was then, Betty. I'm not ready now. I can't do it."

"Yes, ma'am." Betty buttoned her dress. "I'm sorry. I'll get back to my work."

She left the room and Jean lay quietly waiting for her body to stop throbbing. She had wanted that so bad. It was true. It had been too long since she'd had a woman, but she didn't want just any woman. She wanted Maggie. Only Maggie. She dozed into a restless nap filled with erotic images of naked women.

❖

She awoke feeling horny and alone.

She heard the phone ring and knew Betty would answer it. Betty was at her door a minute later.

"It's Mr. Duvall, ma'am."

"I'll be right down."

The cobwebs cleared from her head as she walked downstairs.

"Hello, David."

"Hello, Jean. Are you okay? You sound a bit down."

"I'm fine. I just woke up from a nap."

"Well, take a shower and get dressed. The cast party is in an hour and I'm sending a car for you."

"I don't know, David..."

"You don't know? Jean, it's the star's obligation to be there. It would be scandalous if you didn't show up."

"That's all I need is more scandal," Jean said. "Fine. I'll get ready."

Jean put on her red cocktail dress and matching red pumps. She touched up her makeup and was finally ready just as Betty called up that her car was there.

She was still not in the mood for the party. She knew David was right. Her attendance was required. The driver opened the door of her car and she stepped out to flashbulbs going off all around her. She was momentarily blinded and lost her footing. There was a strong hand at her elbow keeping her steady.

"Easy, darling." She heard Arthur's voice and fought the urge to yank her arm away, but didn't want to fall.

"Thank you." She smiled at him. The cameras kept going off.

Arthur guided her inside. Just as they entered, he whispered in her ear.

"Don't expect any more favors from me."

"You know," Jean said. "It certainly doesn't hurt you any to be linked with me, either."

"I'm not a faggot. I don't need a cover."

He walked off, leaving her fuming. She barely noticed David walking up.

"Smiles, sweetheart. Act like you're having a good time."

"I just got here and already I'm miserable."

"I saw you walk in with Arthur. I'm sorry. But you two do make a striking couple."

Jean didn't say anything.

"Come, dear. Let's get you some champagne."

He steered her through the crowd to the champagne fountain. She helped herself to a glass. She sipped the cool liquid and felt herself begin to relax. She glanced around the room and saw people chatting and dancing to a string quartet. She took a deep breath. She was Jean Sanders and deserved to be at the party. She worked hard to achieve her status and deserved to revel in the closing of another movie sure to be a success.

She moved through the crowds, head held high, troubles forgotten for the moment. She was treated like royalty by all the attendees. It was a good feeling. She moved thoughts of Maggie out of her head. For that night and that night alone, it was all about her. And she made the most of it.

David had her on the dance floor most of the evening, but she also danced with Arthur and other members of the cast. She felt like she was floating on air. She was relaxing for the first time in months.

MJ WILLIAMZ

As the evening drew to a close, a somewhat tipsy Jean climbed into her car and was driven home. She found Betty waiting for her. She was naked save her stockings. And she sat on one of Jean's overstuffed chairs.

"Betty. You almost gave me a heart attack. What are you doing here?"

"I thought you might want to keep the celebration going."

Jean's brain, foggy with the champagne, tried to recall why she had said no earlier. Betty was beautiful with her lush dark hair and her pouty lips. She took in the sight before her and dropped to her knees.

"Yes, Mistress. Please," Betty said.

Jean kissed the inside of Betty's thigh. She smelled her scent. She craved a woman. It had been too long.

The fog lifted, and Jean realized she didn't crave just any woman. She craved Maggie.

"No." She stood. "I told you it's not right and I meant it. Now leave."

"But, Mistress. I've missed you so."

"It won't happen, Betty. Not now. Not ever again. I need you to get dressed and go home. It's late. And I won't need you here tomorrow. Take a day off."

"But…"

"No. Good night, Betty."

❖

The following morning, Jean was in the kitchen when the phone rang.

"Hello?"

"Hello. Is this Jean Sanders?"

• 146 •

"It is. Who's calling please?"

"My name is Thomas O'Leary. I'm with the House Committee on Un-American Activities. I'd just like to ask you a few questions. Is there a good time to meet somewhere?"

Jean felt bile rising in her throat. She didn't want to talk to Thomas O'Leary, but knew if she didn't it would look even worse. She knew he'd ask her questions about Maggie, and she had to steel herself for the discussion. She shouldn't worry, she cautioned herself. She was an actress. She'd just play the role of her lifetime, a straight actress with no knowledge of any homosexuals in Hollywood.

"Sure. I'll be happy to meet with you. I've just woken up. Can we meet for lunch at noon?"

"That would be fine. I'll meet you at The Well. Are you familiar with that place? No one should bother us there."

"Sounds good. I'll see you then."

She took a deep breath and went upstairs to shower. The butterflies in her stomach were fluttering madly. She thought she might be sick. She briefly contemplated calling The Well and leaving a message that she couldn't make it. That would solve things. Temporarily. The reality was, O'Leary was in town and she had to accept it.

She called David.

"Hello?"

"David? It's Jean."

"To what do I owe this pleasure?"

"Guess who I'm having lunch with today?"

"I have numerous guesses, but I don't trust the phone, so why don't you tell me?"

"Thomas O'Leary."

"*The* Thomas O'Leary?"

"The one and only. Oh, David. I'm so scared."

"Be calm. He doesn't have any facts. He's just fishing for information. Don't give him any."

"I won't, David. You know that."

"I do know that, Jean. I know he'll press you hard, but you'll hold up."

"Okay. I need to get going. I'll talk to you this afternoon."

"Good luck."

She hung up the phone and noticed her hand was shaking. She needed to make that stop. She could show no outward signs of nerves. The rest would be easy.

Jean arrived at The Well a few minutes early. She had no idea what O'Leary would look like. While she had heard of the man, she'd never paid him enough mind to look into him. Surely he'd been in newspapers, but she only read the reviews in the papers. The rest of the world was too dismal to deal with.

"Miss Sanders?" She turned to see a short, dark-haired man in black rimmed glasses.

"Mr. O'Leary?"

"Please, call me Thomas."

"Fine, Thomas."

"I've got us a booth over in the corner. We should be free from prying eyes."

"I certainly hope so."

"Right. You wouldn't want to be seen with the man trying to clean up Hollywood, after all."

"Not everybody agrees that's what you're doing. Many call it a witch-hunt. And you're right, I don't need to be seen with you. I've had enough bad press lately."

"Well, I'm not on a witch-hunt. I assure you. I am trying to get the communists and homosexuals out of Hollywood to return it to the wholesomeness it once had."

"Which is why we think it's a witch-hunt. I've been in Hollywood for years, and I know no communists nor homosexuals."

"Let's talk about Margaret Cranston."

Jean felt her stomach curdle. She cautioned herself to remain calm.

"Let's."

"She was living with you for several months."

"Yes, she was."

"Did you know at the time that she was a known communist sympathizer?"

What? Where did they get their information? She knew he was fishing. She told herself not to react.

"I did not know that. She didn't mention communism ever to me."

"You're telling me in all the time you two were together, she never confided in you."

"I'm not sure what you mean by together, but in all the time I've known her, no."

"She's also a known homosexual. Surely you knew that," he said.

"I'd have no reason to ever suspect her of that. While she was living with me, she only dated men."

"Just as you do."

"Just as I do."

"You've been seen a lot with Arthur Langdon. He's a straight up guy. You should see him more. It's good for your image."

"Who I date is really none of your business, Mr. O'Leary."

"It is if it's Margaret Cranston."

"I've already said there was nothing between us."

"No," he said. "You never did say that."

"Well, I'm saying it now."

"I plan to talk to her, as well. Just so you know," he said. "You may as well tell me the truth. I'll get it out of her if you won't confess."

"You just said you know I've been seeing Arthur Langdon." She was irritated and frustrated. She hated the way he tried to scare her into admitting something that was none of his damned business.

"Let's switch gears here. Tell me what you know of Dorothy Martin."

Jean was caught completely off guard. She hoped her face didn't give anything away.

"What about her?"

"You've starred with her in movies."

"Yes, I have."

"It's common knowledge that she passes out communist pamphlets on the set. Did you read yours?"

"She never gave me anything of the sort."

"Tell me, Miss Sanders. How can you live in the midst of all of this and associate with active homosexuals and communists and be so completely unaware? Either you're naïve, stupid, or lying."

"I don't need to take this from you." Jean stood.

"Please, sit. I only have a few more questions."

"Fine." She sat back down and eyed O'Leary suspiciously. "Only don't insult me again. I'm neither stupid nor am I a liar."

"I'm sorry," he said. "It's just that I know you have to know something. I just wish you'd share it with me. It'll make it a lot easier on you in the future. The last person I want to ask you about today is your dear friend David Duvall. He's an admitted homosexual, so you can't deny that."

"I can and I will." She knew David was not open about his sexuality for just this reason. She had pretty much lost all patience with Mr. O'Leary.

"I do believe he's affiliated himself rather openly with Spencer Roberts."

Jean felt the sweat beading on her forehead. She licked her dry lips.

"I know nothing of the sort. David and I are more of an item than they are."

"Not really. You two simply cover for each other."

"Are you accusing me of being a lesbian now?" Jean said.

"Who else lives with a woman for several months?"

"I was her mentor. Her coach. I helped her with her acting. She was like a baby sister to me."

"So why did she move out?"

"You saw the rags, I'm sure. Making wild accusations. Neither of us could afford such scandal in our careers. So we decided she should move out."

"And you've not seen each other since. Sounds more like a breakup."

"We are not seeing each other, as you say, until the dust settles. We have not broken up. There was nothing to break up. We will resume our friendship when sharks like you quit smelling blood in the water. You're all a bunch of perverts seeing things that aren't there, things that are only in your sick minds."

"Oh, I don't think so, Miss Sanders."

"Oh, I know so, Mr. O'Leary."

"Aren't you going to eat your lunch?" He motioned to her plate of untouched food.

"I'll take it to go. I'm not very hungry right now."

"Guilt will do that to you."

Fuck you, she wanted to scream at him.

"I've nothing to feel guilty about. I'm an upstanding American citizen. Heck, I'm America's Sweetheart. You should be ashamed of yourself trying to sully my reputation."

She motioned to the waitress.

"May I get a box, please?"

When the waitress walked away, Jean leaned over the table toward O'Leary.

"Listen. Maybe there are people in Hollywood who do things like you say. I don't know every single person here. But I do know that the circle you're looking into now won't reveal anything. You're barking up the wrong tree. I can assure you of that."

O'Leary stood. He threw a wad of cash on the table.

"I don't think so, Miss Sanders. And it's just a matter of time before the shell cracks and the truth comes out."

She was visibly shaking by the time she left the restaurant. She did her best to calm her nerves, but she was too upset. She got in her car and drove home, where she immediately called David.

CHAPTER NINE

D avid answered on the second ring.

"David? Oh, my God. That was horrible."

"Jean? Shh. The phones have ears. I'll be there in just a few minutes."

True to his word, David arrived in less than ten minutes. He took one look at Jean's puffy, red eyes and pulled her to him.

"Oh Lord, Jean. What happened?"

Jean proceeded to tell him about the inquisition, as she called it.

"It was horrible," she said. "They know about Maggie and me, of course, but they also know about you and Spencer."

"No," David said. "They don't know anything. I told you. They're fishing. And if you didn't give them anything, then that's a point for our side."

"But what if they ask someone else? What if they question Arthur? Oh, God, David."

"They will. You know that. We just have to stand strong in our denials."

"David, I don't want to go to jail."

"Oh, darling. You're not going to jail. None of us are. They are simply trying to scare people. And if people get scared enough, they admit things. But we won't get that scared, will we?"

"No. Never. I will protect Maggie until my dying day."

"And me, too, I hope." David laughed.

"Of course you too."

"Now rest up," David said. "We start filming *Summer Passion* on Monday."

"I'm so excited to be working with Maggie," Jean said.

"Jean, you mustn't get your hopes up. Maggie had a terrible scare, too. And she doesn't have the support system you do. So don't expect her to welcome you back with open arms. If anything, I anticipate more tension on the set than you had with Arthur."

"Oh, David. Don't say that. We'll be fine. We'll be so happy to be together again."

"Be careful, Jean. Protect your heart. I don't want to see you hurt again."

"She won't hurt me, David. She loves me."

"Just be careful. I should go now and you should rest. You've had a stressful day."

"Thanks for coming over." She hugged him.

"My pleasure. Now don't you give that Thomas O'Leary a second thought and I'll see you Monday morning."

Jean was used to having a longer break between pictures, but she wasn't going to complain about filming back-to-back movies since it meant she would be with Maggie every day. She couldn't wait.

❖

Monday morning, she woke early, full of excitement. Not only would she be working with Maggie, but her costar was Spencer Roberts, with whom she got along very well. No more Arthur Langdon to deal with. Although she supposed it would be awkward to kiss Spencer in front of David and Maggie, but it was all acting and they were professionals.

She showered, applied a light layer of makeup and drove to the lot. The butterflies in her stomach were back, but this time not from fear. She couldn't wait to see Maggie. She practiced what to say to her. She imagined she would simply take her in her arms and hold her close, smelling the aroma that was Maggie's alone.

When she walked onto the set, David was alone.

"Where is everyone?" She asked.

"In their dressing rooms. Which is where you should be. Your makeup artist is in there already waiting for you."

Jean walked into her dressing room, her heart pounding. It was almost time to see Maggie. She sat as still as she could while her makeup was applied. When she was dressed and ready, she stepped back onto the set. She saw Maggie talking to David. Her heart stopped. She gazed at her figure and her beautiful, shiny hair, and her palms began to sweat.

She crossed the set and placed her hand on Maggie's shoulder. She turned and their gazes met.

"Maggie. It's so good to see you."

"Hello, Jean."

"How have you been?"

"Good. Really good. You?"

"I'm doing okay."

"Ladies," David said. "Let's get filming."

Jean focused on her lines and Spencer was spot on in his. The first day went smoothly and without a hitch. After David called it a day, Jean sought out Maggie again.

"Maggie, would you like to go have dinner?" she asked.

"That wouldn't be wise."

"Sure it would. We'll get David and Spencer to come along."

"Thanks, but no. I'm not ready. I should go get into my street clothes. I'll see you tomorrow."

Jean tried to hide her disappointment.

"Yeah. I'll see you tomorrow."

Jean went to her dressing room and lit a smoke. She took a long drag and exhaled. She closed her eyes. It had been a good day, overall. She had had to concentrate hard to hit her lines and not focus on Maggie all the time. That had been draining, but she'd done it. The first day of shooting was a wrap and she knew now she could be in the same room as Maggie and still function.

Still, she wished Maggie would have agreed to go out with her. She missed her so. A simple dinner to get caught up would have been nice. She told herself to be patient. Soon, she was sure, Maggie would come around.

She put out her cigarette and took off her makeup. She put her street clothes back on and was on her way to her car when David stopped her.

"Dinner?" he said.

"Sure."

"Let's go to Barichelli's."

"I don't know if I'm in the mood to be in the limelight."

"It'll be good for you," David said. "We'll make a dashing couple."

Jean had to laugh. They did look good together and were seen quite often. The trick was not to let the press know the truth of their relationship.

"You're right," she said. "Let's do this."

As they approached the restaurant from the parking lot, cameras clicked and flashes flashed.

"Did you split up with Arthur Langdon?" someone yelled.

David stopped and made Jean face the throng and answer.

"We are still dear friends," Jean said. "But we are no longer dating."

"What about Mr. Duvall here?" someone else said. "You two are always together."

"A girl never kisses and tells." Jean smiled and allowed David to steer her inside.

"You were wonderful," David said. "Brava, my dear."

"Thank you. I just wish they didn't care who I dated."

"It's their job to keep track of that. It sells, my dear."

"I suppose. I still wish that they discussed our movies and our acting abilities rather than our personal lives."

"That's not as much fun to read. And leads to much less scandal."

"Speaking of scandal," Jean said, "Maggie wouldn't even consider going to dinner with me tonight."

"Give her some time."

"I don't want to give her time. I want her to treat me as more than a costar."

David smiled at her.

"Sweetie, she's scared. And you know in your heart you're more than a costar to her. You *know* that. You need to hold on to that and be patient. She'll come around eventually."

"Eventually. Ugh. I am so tired of waiting."

"Relax now and enjoy your dinner."

"I'll try."

"At least let me believe I'm good company."

Jean chuckled.

"That's better," David said.

"Oh, David, whatever would I do without you?"

"Who knows, my dear? Who knows?"

Jean was able to finally decompress after a glass of wine. She felt mellow and at ease and chatted easily with David.

"How did you think the first day of shooting went?" Jean said.

"I think it went well. I think we need to feel more chemistry between you and Spencer and less between you and Maggie, though."

"You can't be serious. I'm a professional, David. My feelings for Maggie aren't showing."

"I hate to say it, but they are. I don't know how to put it. But there's a force between you two. You're like two magnets, and when I'm filming I can see that invisible force drawing you to each other."

"But surely you sense something between Spencer and myself, even if it's not there."

"I didn't too much today. It wasn't bad. I mean, not enough to reshoot, but I'd like to feel it more. You both probably need to work at it. I know it's not all you."

"No, I'm sure he's more into you than me. Unfortunately, my attentions are directed toward someone on screen. It's harder to hide."

"True. Just work on it. That's all I'm asking. Outside of that, I think today went very well."

❖

Shooting continued going well for the next couple of weeks. Jean took David's advice to heart and focused completely on Spencer when they had scenes, rather than on Maggie. Maggie was a true artist, and Jean learned to appreciate her skills. She knew she'd strike it big someday, sooner rather than later.

"Cut!" David yelled one Friday afternoon. "That's a wrap for today."

As usual, Jean went directly to her dressing room, lit a cigarette, and removed her stage makeup. She heard a knock on her door.

"Who is it?"

"It's Maggie."

Jean opened the door. She couldn't believe her eyes. Maggie was a vision standing there in her street clothes with her makeup lightly done.

"Come on in," Jean said.

"Thanks."

Jean closed the door behind her and could hardly breathe. The close quarters of her dressing room were almost too much to bear. It was painful to be this close to Maggie and not touch her, kiss her, tell her how much she'd missed her.

"What can I do for you?" The words sounded so formal to her own ears.

"I've talked to David and Spencer and they'd like to go out to dinner tonight. I'd love you to join us."

Jean let the words sink in. Dare she read too much into them? She hoped against all hope this was a chance Maggie was taking to get some time with her.

"Sure." She tried to sound nonchalant. "That sounds great." Maggie exhaled.

"Great. See you out there in a few?"

"I'll be there."

Jean hurried to change into her street clothes. Her stomach turned, she was so nervous. She noticed her hands were shaking as she smoothed her skirt. She took a deep breath and stepped out onto the set.

She found the three of them waiting. Spencer and David seemed so relaxed, but Maggie's smile was tight. She hoped they were doing the right thing.

Everyone took their own car and they met at a popular restaurant. In the parking lot, Maggie slipped her hand through Spencer's elbow and Jean slipped her hand through David's. They crossed to the parking lot and before they reached the door, the cameras were all turned to them. They stopped for pictures, all smiles. They paused for several minutes before David opened the door for the rest of the party.

At their table, the men sat across from each other and engaged in conversation, leaving Jean and Maggie on their own.

"So, how've you been?" Jean asked.

"Good. You?"

"Good." She took a sip of wine. "No. That's not true. I've been miserable."

"I'm sorry, Jean. That's why I thought we should do dinner. I mean, I know you suggested this a couple of weeks ago, but I wasn't ready. At this point, I needed to be with you. I miss you so much. I mean, I know I see you every day on the set, but that's different. And we're acting, so we're not being ourselves. I just needed some time to simply be with you."

"I'm glad you decided to do this. I wasn't going to push you, but I have missed you so much. And working together just makes it harder."

"It really does. But we're getting through it okay."

"That's because we're professionals," Jean said.

"We truly are." Maggie laughed. "When this movie comes out and rakes in all that money, we'll be laughing, knowing there was more passion between the lead actress and her supporting actress than with her leading man."

"You are so very right."

"Come over for dinner tomorrow night," Maggie said.

"What?" Jean's heart stopped. Every ounce of her wanted to say yes, but the scandal had finally died down. She didn't want to risk a resurgence.

"Please. The press doesn't camp out at my house. Sure, they'll be at your house, but if you drive around, you can lose anyone who follows you. Please say you'll come over. Please."

Jean considered her options. People of the press seldom followed her once she left her house. They all mostly just wanted to take pictures of her. A few would shout out and ask where she was going, but she could simply ignore them, as usual.

"Okay," Jean said. "I'll come over. That'll be swell. What time?"

"Seven?"

"Sounds great. I'll be there."

"Excellent."

The rest of dinner passed pleasantly. At the end, David was all smiles.

"We should do this again some time."

"We should do this all the time," Jean said.

David laughed.

"I'd love that."

"Okay, so it's settled. Once a week the four of us go out to dinner," Jean said.

"Twice a week," Spencer said.

"Twice a week it is," David said.

The men escorted them back to their cars and hugs were exchanged all around.

"We'll see you at work on Monday," David said.

"See you then," Jean said.

Jean could barely sleep that night. She was too excited about Saturday's dinner with Maggie. She tossed and turned and finally fell asleep holding her pillow, dreaming of Maggie.

❖

Jean dressed in as masculine a fashion as she could get away with. Her skirt was long and straight, her shirt a long sleeve, button down blue cotton. She felt good. She hoped she wasn't getting her hopes up too high, but she really wanted the evening to end with her in Maggie's bed.

She stopped by a florist en route and picked up a nice fall arrangement full of orange lilies, red carnations, and lush greenery. She thought it was a perfect gift.

Jean arrived at Maggie's house at exactly seven o'clock. Her palms were sweating. She felt like a teenager on her first date. She wiped her palms on her skirt as she waited for Maggie to open the door. When Maggie did open it, Jean's heart skipped a beat.

Maggie looked stunning in a green dress that showed off her eyes. Her skin had paled since their trip to Palm Springs and the contrast was breathtaking.

Jean handed her the floral arrangement.

"Thank you," Maggie said. "You didn't have to."

"I didn't want to show up empty-handed."

"That's very thoughtful of you."

Jean was on edge. Every ounce of her wanted to take Maggie in her arms and kiss her. She didn't know how Maggie would feel about that, though, so she kept her distance.

"This is a nice place," she said.

"Thanks. I like it. It's nothing fancy, just a little cottage, but it works for me."

"Will you be buying now that you're becoming a star?"

"I don't know. I kind of like living out of the limelight."

"We both know that won't last for long. You're too good and your career has really taken off."

"Yeah. I feel like *Summer Passion* is really going to launch me into the big time."

"I hope it does, Maggie. I really hope it does."

"I like hearing you say my name," Maggie said.

Jean swallowed hard. Her mouth was dry and her voice crackled.

"You do, huh?"

"I do. I've missed it."

Jean just nodded. Maggie took a deep breath.

"Well, I hope you're hungry. I've made lasagna for dinner. It's almost ready. Would you like a glass of wine?"

"I'd love one."

Jean followed Maggie into the kitchen, admiring the sway of her hips as she walked. Her palms itched to touch her, to caress her. Her head was light with desire and she was almost afraid to be there. Almost.

Maggie handed Jean the decanter and glasses.

"Do you mind?" she said.

"Not at all."

Jean tried to steady her hands as she poured the Cabernet.

"Are you nervous?" Maggie asked.

"I am. I'll be honest. I am a little nervous."

"So am I. Let's take these into the living room where we can relax."

They sat together on the love seat. Jean was in both heaven and hell sitting that close to Maggie.

"I don't know that this is helping," she said.

"I know what you mean." Maggie laughed. "Let's just relax, okay? Tell me, what have you been doing with yourself?"

"Nothing, really. Acting, of course, but that's about it."

"I heard you were seeing Arthur Langdon."

"Oh, my God. That was a disaster. He is such an asshole."

"I wondered. You went out a couple of times, though."

"I tried. I really tried to put up a good front, but he was anything but a gentleman when the cameras weren't around. He tried to force himself on me in his car."

"Oh, Jean. I'm so sorry."

"And then he called me a dyke for not going along with him."

"What a jerk."

"So, yeah. It looks like I'll just settle for David being my steady date."

"That's safe. I've been dating Spencer. He's safe, too."

"Exactly. And we're as good for them as they are for us."

"So anything else new in your world?" Maggie said.

"Actually, yes." Jean set her glass on the coffee table and turned to face Maggie. "Thomas O'Leary came sniffing around me."

"Oh, no. Not *the* Thomas O'Leary?"

"The very one. He was asking all sorts of questions about us and David and Spencer. He even asked me about Dorothy Martin. I realize I might be hurting any chance with you by telling you this, but I thought it only fair you know."

"I appreciate your honesty, Jean. I really don't think Mr. O'Leary can clear out the homosexuals and communists in our city. I'm not worried about him too much. I do, however, still worry about my reputation as a whole."

"I understand that."

"So, we just have to be incredibly secretive, okay?"

"That's fine," Jean said. "I think discretion is key."

"I'm glad we're in agreement. Now, are you ready for some dinner?"

They made their way to the kitchen where Maggie served them.

"This lasagna is amazing," Jean said.

"I'm glad you like it. It's an old family recipe."

"Cranston doesn't sound too Italian."

"No, but Carbini does, no? That was my mother's maiden name."

"That makes good sense then. Well, you're a fabulous cook."

"Thank you."

"That being said," Jean said, "have you ever considered hiring a cook?"

"No way," Maggie said. "I love cooking too much."

"You say that, but wait until you shoot late into the evening and you come home exhausted. It's very nice to have a hot meal waiting for you."

"I'm sure it is," Maggie said. "Maybe that will be something for me to consider in the future."

She stood and began to clear the table.

"Here, let me," Jean said. Her hand slightly brushed Maggie's as they reached for the same plate. She felt the current shoot through her. She wanted Maggie so desperately. She cautioned herself to be calm. Maggie was in charge. She'd follow her lead.

They cleared the table and worked together to get the kitchen clean.

"That's another thing about having help," Jean said. "She'll do the dishes, too."

Maggie laughed.

"I honestly don't mind. I like to feel normal, Jean, you know? I like to have a place I can come and remember who I am."

"I get that. I truly do. But I'd be at a loss without Betty."

"Oh, yeah. I'm sure you would." She laughed. "She does everything for you."

"That she does. But it's so nice and convenient."

"Well, if and when I'm ever ready for that, I'll see if Betty can give me any recommendations."

"Sounds good." They stood in the kitchen, work done. Jean wasn't sure if she should say good night or not. The silence was too much for her.

"How about another glass of wine?" Maggie finally said.

"Sure."

They took their wine into the living room and once again sat on the loveseat. This time Maggie sat close enough to Jean to touch her.

Jean placed her arm around Maggie and pulled her close.

"This is nice," Maggie said.

"Yes, it is," Jean said. "It's wonderful."

"I've missed you so much."

"I've missed you, too.

"Kiss me, Jean? Please?" She turned her face to Jean, tilted her head slightly, and parted her lips.

Jean took in the sight. Her heart raced. She had waited so long for this. She wanted to draw out the moment. She cupped Maggie's face in her hand and dragged her thumb over her jaw and down to her lips. She traced their outline. She gasped when Maggie closed her lips over her thumb and sucked on it. She felt her nipples harden at the sensation.

She moved her thumb away from Maggie's mouth and lowered her own mouth to taste Maggie's lips. They were as soft and sweet as she'd remembered, and she wanted more, so much more.

Jean pried Maggie's lips open with her tongue and tasted the warm wine in Maggie's mouth. She grew dizzier with each passing minute as their tongues frolicked together.

Jean finally sat back and took Maggie's glass of wine. She set both of their glasses on the table and climbed on top of Maggie. She kissed her again, hard, while she leaned her back on the loveseat.

Maggie moved her hands all over Jean's body. Jean felt the heat everywhere they touched. They burned through her clothes, which she wanted to take off. She wanted to lay bare with Maggie and feel their skin against each other.

Jean reached behind Maggie and unzipped her dress. The feel of her soft, warm skin underneath made her crotch clench. She kissed her neck and her chest, craving more with each nibble.

Maggie sat up.

"Come on. Let's go to my room."

"Are you sure?"

"I've never been more sure of anything," Maggie said.

"Lead the way."

Maggie took Jean's hand and led her down the hallway to a large master bedroom. The bed was large and looked quite comfortable. She had a matching dresser and dressing table. It was a very feminine room and Jean had to smile.

"It's so you."

"Thank you. Now, kiss me again."

Jean was happy to oblige. She pulled Maggie close and kissed her passionately on the mouth. Her tongue swirled around the inside of her mouth as she peeled Maggie's dress off her.

It fell to the floor and Maggie stepped out of it. She looked a vision in her undergarments. Jean ran her tongue over the soft mounds of Maggie's flesh that peeked out above her bra. She kissed them and sucked on the silky skin.

"Careful," Maggie said. "We can't have any marks."

"No. Of course not."

Jean eased Maggie back on the bed and climbed on top of her. She peeled her bra straps off her shoulders and kissed every spot her hands touched. She was barely able to maintain control. She wanted Maggie so desperately. She wanted to rip her clothes off and have her way with her. She took a deep breath to steel herself with some self-control.

"Is everything okay?" Maggie asked.

"Everything's fine. Wonderful. I just don't want to go too fast."

"You won't. You can't. I'm ready for this. As ready as you are."

Jean kissed Maggie hard then and showed her the need she was feeling inside. She kissed down her chest and belly and finally sat up to remove Maggie's garters and stockings. As she peeled the stockings off, she licked and sucked her legs, all the way down to her feet.

She stood and quickly undressed before she kissed back up Maggie's legs and stopped when she came to where they met. She gazed at her breathlessly.

"You're beautiful," she said. "Just beautiful."

Jean kissed along one inner thigh and then the other, teasing both Maggie and herself. She breathed in the scent of Maggie and felt the moist heat radiating from her. She didn't know how much more she could take.

She finally lost control and had to taste Maggie. She ran her tongue the length of her, savoring every drop. Maggie was wet and ready for her. She was delicious. Jean had almost forgotten how good she tasted.

She delved her tongue deep inside her, licking every spot she found. Her satin walls felt fantastic against her tongue. She moved her tongue all around, paying special attention to that soft spot she knew drove Maggie wild.

Maggie was holding on to Jean's head, pressing her into her. Her hips pumped as she ground herself into Jean's face. Jean kept up her steady licking until Maggie cried out, and still Jean continued lapping away. She felt Maggie clenching around her, but wasn't ready to stop yet.

Maggie cried out again and again as Jean continued to work her magic. Finally, when she could take no more, she tapped Jean on her shoulder.

"I'm through," she said. "I've got nothing left."

Jean kissed up the length of Maggie's body, loving the rippling of her skin under her kisses. She finally reached her mouth, which she kissed tenderly, lovingly.

Maggie returned her kisses, then increased the pressure on Jean's lips. She pried her mouth open and plunged her tongue inside. She rolled over and pinned Jean beneath her.

"I thought you were wiped out." Jean said when the kiss ended.

"Not completely. Just didn't have any more orgasms in me."

She kissed Jean again and ran her hand down her body. She brought it back to Jean's breast and kneaded it. She squeezed and caressed it until her nipple was rock hard. She pinched the nipple and twisted it as Jean closed her eyes. Maggie continued until Jean shuddered as she reached her first climax.

"That was amazing," she said.

"Good. And we're just getting started."

She moved her hand down Jean's body until she found Jean's swollen clit.

"Oh, you are so ready for me."

"I've never been more ready."

Maggie ran her fingers over Jean's clit. It was slick and warm and she easily slid over it. She pressed it into Jean's pubis as she rubbed it. Jean threw her head back and screamed as she came again.

Still not through, Maggie moved her fingers inside Jean. She stroked her lightly at first and then with added pressure. It took no time for Jean to reach yet another orgasm.

They lay together in bed after, both satiated and basking in the joy of being together.

"I sure do love you," Jean said.

"I love you, too."

"That's good to hear." Jean kissed her forehead.

"But," Maggie said. "Discretion is still key, so you're going to have to leave now."

"Now? But don't I get to hold you?"

"I don't know about you, but if I lay in your arms, where I feel so safe and so comfortable, I'm going to fall fast asleep. And it wouldn't do for you to go home tomorrow morning wearing the same clothes you left in tonight."

"Good point. But I'm thoroughly enjoying the afterglow with you."

"As am I. But, reality is reality, Jean. And if we're going to do this, we need to be extremely careful."

"You're right."

She picked her clothes off the floor and dressed in silence.

"I'll see you Monday?" Jean said.

"Yes, ma'am. And we'll have to play it cool."

"I understand. We will. We'll make this work."

Jean kissed Maggie good night then walked out into the cool night air.

❖

Monday at work was difficult for Jean. She missed a couple of lines when she was thinking about Maggie instead of the movie.

"Take ten," David called. "Jean, a word, please."

"I'm sorry, David."

"I'm sure you are. But I can't have you messing up like that. We've had to retake that scene three times. That's not like you. Where's your head today?"

"I'm sorry. I'm trying to focus. It's just really hard."

"Look, Jean." David lowered his voice. "If this is because we all went out Friday and you got some time with Maggie… well, we just won't be able to do that again. I can't have you missing lines. You're the star here. You should be setting an example."

"That's not what it is. I promise. I'll focus more this afternoon. I promise."

"You'd better."

He called everybody back together.

"From the top," he said.

Jean focused hard on her lines. She told herself she'd have time with Maggie again and that Saturday wasn't a onetime thing. This helped her focus and on that take she was right on the mark with her lines. The rest of the day went smoothly, and they were done by four o'clock.

"That's a wrap for today," David said. "Good work, everybody."

Jean made her way to her dressing room and lit her cigarette. There was a knock on the door.

"Who is it?" she called.

"It's Maggie."

"Come in."

Maggie opened the door and stepped into the room. She crossed it and threw her arms around Jean. She kissed her hard on her mouth. Jean was surprised at first, but then relaxed into the kiss.

"That was nice," she said. "To what do I owe that?"

"I've wanted to do that all day," Maggie said.

"As have I. I was totally distracted today, as you could see."

"I was too, but fortunately, I didn't have a lot of lines today."

"I need to keep it together. David thinks it was because we all went out Friday. I didn't tell him about Saturday."

"Good. The less people who know, the better."

"True. But you know I'll tell him eventually. He's my best friend."

"If you must. I won't be upset. Simply because he's David."

"Right. Thank you."

"Okay," Maggie said. "I should go get changed. I'll see you tomorrow."

Jean walked out of her dressing room to find David lingering.

"Drinks, my dear?" he said.

"Sure."

"We'll take my car. That way we can chat on the way."

Jean felt a cold grip in the pit of her stomach. She felt like a child about to be scolded by a parent. But there was little she could do. She had already agreed to go.

"You really got it together there at the end of the day," David said.

"I did. I'm sorry I was so out of focus this morning."

"Well, that's why we're driving together, so we can talk. I don't trust the phones in this city and you never know who's listening at a restaurant, so tell me, if it wasn't Friday night, then what were you so distracted about today?"

"It was Saturday night," Jean said.

"What was Saturday night?"

"I went to Maggie's for dinner."

"I see," David said.

"It was really nice. So that was why I was distracted. But I pulled myself together, and you have to admit I was spot-on the rest of the day."

"Yes, you were. Okay. Fair enough. Just please be careful."

"I will. We will."

They arrived at a local watering hole and paused for pictures.

"This is good," David said. "As often as we're seen together, there can't be doubt in anyone's mind we're dating."

"I hope you're right. So, how are you and Spencer doing?"

"We enjoyed dinner the other night. I think double dating a couple of times a week will be a really good thing for all of us."

"I think you're right. It can establish us and them as couples."

"It can and it will. I'm sure of it."

❖

The next two days passed with smooth filming, and they finished Wednesday ahead of schedule. To celebrate, they all went out to dinner that night.

The cameras loved them as they posed in front of the restaurant. The flashes went off and they all smiled, genuine smiles since they were four very happy people.

They were seated and the men started up their conversation.

"It's been a good week, hasn't it?" Jean said to Maggie.

"It has been. It's such a joy working with you, both professionally and personally."

"Aw, thank you, Maggie. It's wonderful working with you. You've got some real talent. I'm sure you'll be the star very soon."

"Do you really think so? Because I truly believe I can do it. I mean that. I think I can play a lead."

"I do, too. And I'm sure *Summer Passion* will be the film that catapults you into that role."

Occasionally, the men would join in their conversation and they'd talk about the filming or any Hollywood gossip, but for the most part, each couple kept to themselves. It was a wonderful dinner. Jean was sad to see it end.

"Okay, everyone," David said as they walked back to the parking lot. "Early to bed. We've got a long day ahead of us tomorrow."

"It won't be a long day," Spencer said. "We'll nail every scene and be done early."

"I hope you're right, darling," David said.

Hugs were given all around. When Jean hugged Maggie, she whispered in her ear.

"I love you."

"I love you, too."

❖

The next day on the set, everyone was in a great mood, as was to be expected. Jean loved the arrangement they had. If only she could make love to Maggie more, life would be perfect.

Filming was almost perfect that day with only one scene that had to be reshot. It was a serious scene between Jean and Spencer, ending in a passionate kiss. David wasn't satisfied with the kiss. It took three tries before he called it a wrap.

"What was wrong with that kiss today?" Jean asked when the day ended.

"It just didn't feel right," David said.

"A gay man and a lesbian kissing? How could that not feel right?" She laughed.

"I know. But I needed to feel the kindling there. I needed to know there was a fire between the two characters. It took three tries to get that."

"I'm sorry if I did anything wrong. I really was trying."

"It's okay. It's part of the business. And getting the perfect kiss is one of the hardest things to shoot."

"I understand. Okay, I'm off to change."

She went to her dressing room and had just changed when Maggie knocked on the door.

"It's me. Can I come in?"

"Please do."

Maggie crossed the small room and took Jean's face in her hands. She bent to kiss her, softly at first, but soon the kiss heated up, leaving Jean dizzy with need.

"What was that for?" Jean asked.

"To show you what a real kiss is after a day of kissing Spencer."

"Well, I appreciate that very much," Jean said. "Thank you. May I have more?"

Maggie seemed happy to oblige, she kissed Jean with fervor. Jean returned the kiss in kind. She pulled Maggie onto her lap and caressed her breasts through her blouse.

"Dear God, I want you," Jean said.

"I know, darling. I know. Saturday night again?"

"If I make it that long."

"You will. We will."

"Lord, but it's so hard."

"It is. But we must endure," Maggie said.

"If you don't want me to take you right here, you'd better leave."

"You look like you're ready to leave, too. Walk out with me?"

"Of course."

They left the set together and were immediately photographed.

"Can't they leave us alone?" Maggie said.

"They won't. You know that. But we're not doing anything worth gossiping about. Costars walk off the set together all the time."

They reached their cars and Jean looked around. There were still photographers with their cameras pointed at them.

"I'd hug you good-bye, but I don't think that would be wise," she said.

"No. Good night, Jean."

"Good night."

CHAPTER TEN

The rest of the week flew by. Filming was way ahead of schedule, and they were all jovial when they went to dinner Friday night. As they entered the restaurant, a journalist called out.

"Is it official now? Are you the two new power couples in Hollywood?"

They all laughed. Yes, they were, but not how people thought.

"I suppose we are." David put his arm around Jean and pulled her close.

More flashes went off and they entered the restaurant.

Dinner was wonderful, but Jean was a bundle of hormones.

"I can't wait until tomorrow night," she said.

"I wish there was somewhere we could go besides my place," Maggie said.

"Nonsense. Your place is fine."

"But wouldn't it be fun to go out together?"

"I'm sure it would, but I'm much more looking forward to staying in with you."

"So, what's tonight's topic of conversation for you two?" David asked.

Jean blushed and David laughed.

"Okay. Obviously, it's personal. I just hope you two will be careful."

"We have no choice," Maggie said. "Neither of us is willing to jeopardize our careers again."

"Good. I don't want to read a thing about you two in the papers."

"You won't," Jean said. "If there's a single photographer at Maggie's house, I won't go in. It's that simple."

"Thank you. I'd hate to see you two suffering for this."

"We won't," Maggie said.

At the end of dinner, they left the restaurant. David was holding Jean's hand and Spencer Maggie's. They walked to the parking lot together. As Jean climbed into her car, David leaned in.

"I mean it, Jean. Please be extra vigilant. Thomas O'Leary and his ilk are not to be taken lightly."

"I understand, dear. I'll be careful."

❖

Saturday morning, Jean awoke bright and early, full of excitement. This time they had decided she should be there at five rather than seven, giving them two more hours together. To pass the time, she read from her script, practicing her lines. She had quite a few scenes with Maggie the following week and she wanted to be sure she could say her lines without the love and passion she felt for her coming through.

Three o'clock rolled around and Jean stepped into a warm bubble bath. She poured in some musk oil and lit some candles. She was perfectly relaxed. Well, almost. She was anxious to see Maggie.

She managed to soak for half an hour, and got out just as her fingers were beginning to prune. Once out, she dried off and applied what little makeup she needed to keep the press happy. She wished she didn't have to wear any, but that wasn't the case. She had an appearance to keep up.

She dressed again in a straight skirt and button down blouse, this one lavender. She looked in the mirror and thought she looked fine for press photos as well as looking good for Maggie.

Finally, it was time to leave. She walked out to find the usual photographers waiting outside. She smiled and waved as she made her way to her car. She stopped and picked up a bottle of wine to take to Maggie's.

When she arrived, Maggie opened the door wearing nothing but a short black satin robe.

"You look breathtaking," Jean said. "But aren't you a little overdressed?"

Maggie laughed.

"I was going to get all dolled up for you, but then thought this might do the trick."

"It does."

Jean closed the door behind her and pulled Maggie into her arms. She kissed her with all her pent up passion as she deftly untied the robe and slid it to the floor. She walked Maggie back to the couch and leaned her onto it. She climbed on top of her and kissed her face and neck before kissing her lips again.

"You need to get out of your clothes," Maggie said.

Jean stood and stripped her clothes off. She tossed them on the ground and climbed back on top of Maggie. The feel of their bare skin together sent shivers throughout her body.

"You smell good," Maggie said.

"So do you." She kissed her again, then moved her mouth down her body. She stopped at a pert breast and took a nipple in her mouth. She barely sucked on it at first. She simply ran her tongue over it.

"Oh, dear God, that feels good," Maggie said.

Jean could wait no longer and pulled Maggie's nipple deep inside her mouth. She sucked on it with all her power and was rewarded with Maggie tangling her fingers in her hair.

"Oh, yes, darling. Yes," Maggie said.

Jean moved her hand to Maggie's free breast and pinched that nipple while she continued to suckle her other.

"Oh, Jesus, Jean. Oh, sweet Jesus," Maggie cried as she climaxed.

"That was just the appetizer," Jean said. "Save the rest for after dinner."

Maggie just lay there staring at her.

"Are you serious?"

"I am. That was just a taste of things to come."

"You sure know how to get a girl worked up," Maggie said.

"That's my job. Now, do you have another robe or something I can wear so I don't have to get all dressed again?"

Maggie padded down the hall and returned with a white terrycloth robe for Jean, who donned it immediately.

"Now," Jean said. "What's for dinner?"

"I thought we'd barbecue some steaks."

"Is that safe?"

"What do you mean?"

"Is it safe? I don't want to be caught in a bathrobe in your backyard."

"My backyard is surrounded by tall trees. And there are no reporters here anyway."

Jean walked out the slider to the backyard. She felt safe.

"Okay. Hand me those steaks and I'll start grilling."

"You don't have to. I mean, I was thinking you could, too, but I can grill and it would make more sense for me to be in my backyard in a robe. So I'll grill."

"I'm sorry, doll. I hate to be paranoid."

"It's okay. I understand. And I agree. I'll grill. You make the salad."

Jean set about her task. She felt much more comfortable hidden inside. The salad was ready just as Maggie brought the steaks inside.

They dined with quiet conversation and enjoyed the wine Jean had brought with her. After dinner, they did the dishes together and soon the kitchen was spotless.

"Gee," Maggie said. "What shall we do now?"

"We should take this show into the bedroom."

"Are you sure?"

"I'm positive. I'm not waiting another minute to have my way with you."

"Sounds good to me."

Jean peeled Maggie's robe off her and quickly removed her own. She climbed onto the bed and pulled Maggie on top of her. Maggie looked radiant above her. Her hair was cascading over her shoulders and teasing Jean with the way it covered her breasts.

"I love your hair." Jean ran her fingers through her silky locks. She wrapped her fingers in them and pulled Maggie to her. Their kiss was passionate and magical, and Jean never wanted it to end. Maggie finally broke the kiss.

"I never want to stop kissing you," Jean said.

"Oh, I know what you mean. I love your kisses."

Jean pulled her back for another seemingly endless kiss. It went on and on, and when it ended, Jean was breathless and needed more. She tried to roll over on top of Maggie, but Maggie held her ground.

"I rather enjoy being on top of you," Maggie said. "It's nice to look down and see the passion in your eyes from here."

"But I want to have my way with you. I can't do that from here."

"Use your imagination," Maggie said.

Jean ran her hands up and down Maggie's sides. The soft skin fueled her fire. She brought her hands to rest on Maggie's breasts. The firm full mounds fit perfectly in her grasp. She caressed each one before pinching the hardened nipples. She tugged and twisted each one and was lost in the feeling of Maggie bobbing up and down on her. She felt something lightly brushing against her clit and looked down to see Maggie masturbating while Jean played with her nipples.

Every time Maggie stroked her own clit, her fingers dipped low enough to tease Jean's.

"Please," she said. "Don't tease me."

"You like that?" Maggie said.

"I do. Very much. But I need more. Don't just tease me."

Maggie went back to touching herself, this time making sure she pressed into Jean's clit as well.

Jean tried to focus on Maggie's nipples, but her concentration waned as her clit swelled and she approached a climax. She arched her hips to meet each of Maggie's touches. She was close, so very close. It was torture. She needed release.

Maggie continued to move up and down on Jean as she rode her own fingers.

"Darling, are you ready?" she said.

"I'm past ready."

"I'm so close."

"So am I. Please, Maggie, let me come."

Maggie stroked faster and faster with more and more pressure until they both screamed and came together.

"That was amazing," Jean said when she could breathe again. "What possessed you to do that?"

"I just thought it would be fun to see if it worked. It felt so good to have you playing with my nipples that I had to touch myself. And then I realized you were right under me and I could rub you, too. That was a lot of fun."

"Yes, it was, doll. You never cease to amaze me."

Maggie moved down Jean's body until she was between her legs. She picked up her knees and placed them on her shoulders and lowered her head to feast on what she found. She lapped up the remnants of Jean's orgasm and worked her tongue over every spot, encouraging Jean's arousal.

She moved her mouth to Jean's clit and sucked it into her mouth. She licked all over it as she held it between her lips. Jean squirmed on the bed as she began to lose awareness of anything except Maggie. She closed her eyes as the darkness came over her. She saw nothing and felt nothing but Maggie's mouth.

Soon an array of lights lit up her inner eyelids as the orgasms washed over her, cascading through her body one after another.

Maggie lay down next to Jean and held her close. Jean put her arm around her and thought how right everything felt.

"I hate to say this, but I think it's time for you to leave," Maggie said.

"Already?"

"Yes. You can't stay here too late."

"Just once I'd like to spend the night with you. You know, wake up with you and have coffee and relax and spend the next day with you, as well."

"I know, darling. I'd like that, too. But it's not possible. You know that."

"I do. Okay, I'll get going."

She kissed Maggie and climbed out of bed. She wandered down the hall and put her clothes on. She was tired and groggy from their lovemaking, but knew that Maggie was right. She couldn't sleep there.

Maggie followed her to the door. Jean turned and pulled Maggie into a tender hug. She kissed her softly.

"I'll see you Monday."

"I can't wait."

❖

Filming on Monday went extremely well. At the end of the day, David commended all the cast members for their hard work.

"This is by far the most cohesive group I've ever worked with. Thank you all for being professionals and making this so easy and fun to film."

Jean smiled as she walked to her dressing room. She lit a cigarette and waited for Maggie. Surely she would come in. Five minutes passed, then ten. She finished removing her makeup and changed her clothes. She walked out onto the set and found David still in his chair.

"Where's Maggie?" she asked.

"She and Spencer went to dinner. Would you like to go get something?"

"I don't know if I'm in the mood."

"Trouble in paradise?"

"I don't think so. But then she didn't come to my dressing room today."

"She can't do that every day, Jean. It's too easy to start gossip. And she needs to be seen with Spencer as often as possible."

"I understand. It's just so nice when she does come by. I miss her during the week. I mean, I see her every day, but I miss holding her, touching her, kissing her."

"I know what you mean, believe me. I know exactly what you mean. Now let's go get something to eat."

"As often as we go out, I'm beginning to wonder why I need Betty anymore."

"You might not soon. There's something I want to talk to you about."

"What's that?"

"We'll talk over dinner."

They arrived at the restaurant and were seated at their usual table. After they'd ordered, David set a small box on the table. The cameras started going off.

"Jean, I've been thinking," he said. "We get along so well and we need each other so much."

"David, you're scaring me."

"Don't be afraid. Think of the security. Think of the peace it could afford us."

"Are you doing what I think you're doing?"

"Yes. Jean Sanders, will you marry me?"

"Are you serious?" she whispered. "You know I can't do this."

"I know you can and you should. What better cover for us? All of us. And I believe Spencer is proposing to Maggie right now."

Jean's stomach was in knots. She didn't want to be married. Not to anyone, not even David. But he made some valid points. If she was David's wife, rumors would cease. No more questions would arise. It was actually a brilliant solution.

"Yes, David," she said loudly. "I'd love to be your wife."

Flashes went off all around them as he took the ring out of the box and slipped it on her finger.

"Well, I guess we know what will be making headlines in *The Wag* this week," he said.

"And I'd much rather see this than Maggie and me."

"Who wouldn't?"

"So, you really think Spencer is proposing tonight?"

"He's supposed to. We had it all planned out. We'd like to get a ranch together outside of town where both couples can live comfortably."

"You really have put a lot of thought into this. So, when's the big day?"

"That we haven't decided. But it should be sooner rather than later."

"And what kind of wedding will we have?" she asked.

"That will be up to you," he said. "We can have a small, intimate affair or a big Hollywood gala. That's your call."

"Can we have a double wedding?"

"I don't see why not. That's up to you and Maggie. It's your wedding. Your big day."

"Wow, David. I don't know how to thank you. This is genius."

"Thank you. I thought it was pretty brilliant."

The rest of dinner went as usual, but Jean couldn't stop staring at the diamond on her hand. It looked so out of place on her usually empty finger.

On their way out of the restaurant, more flashbulbs lit up.

"When's the wedding?" someone shouted.

"We don't know that yet. When we do, we'll let you know."

"How did he ask you?" someone else said.

"He told me how special I was to him and how wonderful we are together. It was very romantic." Jean was proud of her acting skills. It paid to be a star.

❖

After dinner, Jean drove home lost in thoughts about her upcoming nuptials. As soon as she got home, she called Maggie.

"Hello?"

"Maggie?"

"Jean?"

"How was dinner?" she said.

"It was interesting. Why do you ask?"

"Because David proposed to me tonight and told me Spencer was proposing to you, as well. So, did he?"

"He did. What did you say to David?"

"I said yes. It's wonderful, Maggie. What did you say?"

"I told him yes, too. Oh, Jean, I'm so relieved you said yes, too."

"And David said we could get a ranch outside of town and all live together."

"That's what Spencer said, too. How wonderful would that be?"

"Okay, well, I'd better go. O'Leary and his men are supposedly listening in to our conversations and I think we've said enough for now."

"I agree. Sweet dreams, Jean. I'll see you tomorrow."

Thursday morning, *The Wag* came out with the news of both engagements. Five pages were dedicated to the stories. It was all anyone on the set was talking about. Congratulations were tossed all around.

"Come on, people. I know it's big news and we're all excited, but we have filming to do," David finally said. "Let's get ready to shoot."

After another day of successful filming, Jean slipped into her dressing room and soon after heard a knock on her door.

"Who is it?"

"It's me," Maggie said.

"Come on in."

Maggie walked in and closed the door behind her. She crossed the room and took Jean in her arms. She kissed her hard then rested her head on her shoulder.

"We're doing the right thing, aren't we?" Maggie said.

Jean stroked her back.

"Yes, we are, doll. We're absolutely doing the right thing. This is the smartest thing we could have done."

"I just want to be with you."

"And you will. We'll live together on the ranch. We'll have our own wing and they'll have theirs. We'll appear in public as often as we need to, but we'll mostly be homebodies. Maggie, I love you and I'm excited to be doing this."

"I hope you're right."

"I am. Trust me."

Chapter Eleven

Once the society pages printed the news, Jean couldn't keep up with the phone calls and congratulatory notes. Celebrities seldom paid much heed to *The Wag* unless it was a bad story about them, but the society pages were the Gospel.

They were all at dinner one night.

"I think we should start making wedding plans," Jean said.

"I told you," David said. "That's your thing. You two do all that. Spencer and I will just show up."

Jean leveled a stare at David.

"Don't tell me you wouldn't love picking out flowers and dresses and all the stuff that goes with a wedding."

David blushed.

"I suppose I would, but it's your day, Jean. I'll let you do it."

"Well, first of all, are we having a double wedding or two individual weddings?"

"I vote for a double wedding," Maggie said.

"Me, too," Spencer said. "I think it's just what Hollywood needs to see. Two happy couples getting married together."

"Okay, now that that's settled," David said. "What size wedding are we thinking about having?"

They were all silent for a few moments until Jean spoke up.

"I say we go all out. I mean, money really isn't an object if we're all pitching in. Let's have the biggest wedding Hollywood's ever seen."

"I don't know," Spencer said. "A quiet intimate affair might be nice, too."

"I'm more with Jean," David said. "The more witnesses, the better."

"I guess that's two to one so far. What do you say, Maggie?" Jean said.

"I'm torn," Maggie said. "I'd much prefer a quiet affair, but I understand the need for a lot of witnesses. I guess it would be kind of fun to throw a huge Hollywood bash."

"Of course it would," Jean said.

"Okay then. Let's do a huge Hollywood wedding."

"Fine," Spencer said. "If that's what you two want. As David said earlier, you two do the planning and we just show up."

"We might enlist your help for some things," Jean said.

"And we'll be happy to help," David said, which earned him a sidelong glance from Spencer. "Oh, chin up, darling. It will be fun."

"If you say so," Spencer said.

"Now, when are we getting married?" Jean said. "Normally, we wait a year, but I say we get married sooner. I'm chomping at the bit."

"I agree," David said. "How about six months?"

They all agreed that six months would be perfect. Jean and Maggie would order the invitations that weekend. It was all starting to come together.

That Saturday, Jean went over to Maggie's early. As she left her house, she posed for photographs and told reporters she was going to make wedding plans. Everyone seemed happy to hear that, and Jean got out with no questions about her relationship with Maggie.

She arrived at Maggie's house and Maggie looked stunning in a skirt and blouse. She had very little makeup on. Yet she dazzled.

"You are so beautiful." Jean took her in her arms. "I'm so lucky you're mine."

"I think I'm the lucky one."

"No, it's me. Now if I can only remember not to say 'I do' when it's Spencer's turn at the wedding, we'll be okay."

Maggie laughed.

"I think you'll remember. Oh, can you imagine the scandal if you did that?"

"I know. I won't do it, but I'll be thinking it."

"As will I, my love."

"So, we need to go order invitations and start figuring out who we want to invite."

"Let's get going. I certainly want to do other things besides work on the wedding today," Maggie said.

"I do like the sound of that," Jean said.

They went to the stationery store and ordered their wedding invitations. The woman at the store nearly fainted when they walked in. She was clearly starstruck. They thought she might stop breathing when she learned they were buying invitations for their double wedding.

Jean kept up a pleasant smile, but all she wanted to do was tell the woman to pull herself together.

The invitations ordered, they drove to several bakeries and florists, looking for just the right cakes and flower arrangements.

"Let's go home," Jean said. "We can decide these things later. I'm exhausted."

"Okay. But we need to make decisions, darling."

"I know. I'm just tired right now and feel my fuse getting short. I don't want to embarrass myself or you in public."

"I see. Okay, we'll go."

They got home and sat on the sofa.

"Are you feeling better?" Maggie asked.

"I am. Sorry about that. I was hot and tired and suddenly no longer in the mood."

"It's okay. We all have days like that. Here, lie back and put your head in my lap. I'll soothe you."

"I'm fine," Jean said.

"I think it'll help."

"Okay." Jean lay flat on the couch with her head supported by Maggie's thighs. She closed her eyes as Maggie stroked her hair.

She woke disoriented.

"Well, hello there, darling," Maggie said.

"How long was I asleep?" She shook the cobwebs from her head.

"About an hour. How do you feel?"

"Much better. Thanks for that nap."

"My pleasure," Maggie said.

"Speaking of pleasure," Jean said. "Why not head down the hall and enjoy each other?"

"Are you sure you're in the mood?"

"I'm positive."

They walked down the hall hand in hand. Jean felt like she was where she belonged when she felt Maggie's hand in hers.

"I love you so much," she said.

"I love you, too."

"Show me, Maggie. And let me show you."

"Gladly."

They fell onto the bed together. They kissed and stroked each other for what seemed an eternity when Jean finally stood.

"We need to get out of these clothes."

Maggie stood as well and worked quickly at undressing Jean who was undressing her, as well.

When they were naked, they climbed into bed and Jean kissed every inch of Maggie's body. She left no part untouched. Face, breasts, legs, and everything in between. She worshiped Maggie's body and wanted to be sure Maggie knew it.

When Maggie could take no more teasing, Jean brought her to one orgasm after another.

"You're amazing," Maggie said. "Simply amazing."

"I just love your body."

"I'm glad. It sure loves you, darling."

Maggie returned the favor, loving all of Jean's body. She craved her and couldn't get enough of her. It took little time for Jean to climax over and over again. Satisfied and happy, Maggie climbed up into Jean's arms.

They napped together for several hours then got up and dressed.

"Can we go out for dinner?" Jean asked.

"Do you think that would be a good idea?"

"Sure. A couple of gals planning their wedding over a nice steak. Why not?"

"Okay. Let's do that. I'd love to go out with you."

"We just need to be sure we watch how we look at each other," Jean said.

"That's true. We have to act like we're in love with our fiancés, not each other."

They went to dinner, with lots of pictures taken of them. They told reporters they were working on their wedding plans, which fed the frenzied photographers.

After dinner, they went back to Maggie's house and made love for another couple of hours. It was getting late and Jean had to get dressed to leave.

"I don't want to go home," she said.

"I don't want you to go home."

"I can't wait until we all live in the same house and we can be together all the time."

"I know. As soon as we're married it's going to happen," Maggie said. "And that's only six months away."

"Six months. I can make it that long."

She kissed Maggie good-bye and drove home.

The next few weeks passed, and Jean and Maggie made a list. They planned to send out invitations to everyone they could think of. They would send out over five hundred. Jean was getting more excited with each passing day.

David helped them pick out the flowers and the dresses.

"Oh, darlings, we simply must have a pink and white wedding," he told them.

"Pink and white?" Jean said. "I'm not really the pink type."

"You'll be wearing white. The flowers will be pink and white. It will be simply stunning."

"If you say so," Maggie said.

"We can wear black tuxes with pink carnations. We'll look so dapper."

Jean had to laugh.

"Fine, David. If that's what you want."

"It is."

David helped Jean and Maggie design their dresses. They were extravagant with white lace bodices and long, flowing trains. A few weeks before the wedding, they went in for fittings. They sat in the parking lot before going in.

"I really shouldn't see you in your dress before the wedding," Jean said.

"That's funny," Maggie said. "I'm not marrying you."

"Yes, you are. Don't think for a minute that you're not."

"Oh, Jean. I love you so much."

"I love you too. Okay, let's go in and try these on."

Jean's breath caught at the sight of Maggie in her gown. It took all her self control not to cross the room and kiss her.

"You look beautiful," she said. "Actually, that's an understatement. There's no word to describe how breathtaking you are."

One seamstress went to work fitting Maggie's dress while Jean tried hers on. She felt like a fool in all the frills, but she just told herself it was another role she was playing. She could pull it off with no problem. And the end result was well worth it.

"Wow," Maggie said. "Just wow. You make a stunning bride."

"Why, thank you."

The other seamstress fitted Jean's gown. She took it in in the waist and let it out in the bust.

Soon, they were both happy with what the seamstresses planned to do and made plans to come back in a week to try the dresses on again.

When they were back in the car, Maggie told Jean how much fun she'd been having.

"I know the details are a bit of a pain in the rear, but I've enjoyed spending all this time with you."

"It really has been wonderful being together with you all the time without having to worry about anybody thinking anything about it."

"I know. And just think, in a couple of weeks, we'll be together always."

"I know. I can't wait."

❖

Jean's spirits were dampened the next morning when she got a call from Thomas O'Leary.

"What can I do for you?" she said.

"Meet me for lunch."

"Why?"

"I want to talk to you. We have so much to discuss. I told you I'd be in touch. And now I am."

"Fine. I'll meet you at The Well at noon."

Jean wore dark glasses again and had a scarf around her head. She didn't want to be seen talking to the most hated man in Hollywood.

"What do you want from me?" she said.

"Invite me to your wedding."

"Are you crazy? I'm doing no such thing."

"Invite me or I'll dig into your little convenient wedding."

"What's that supposed to mean?" Jean said.

"It means I know David Duvall is a homosexual. I believe you might be, too. I find it hard to believe you two are getting married for any reason other than to provide covers for each other. If you do not invite me, I will expose this wedding as the sham it is."

"My wedding is not a sham. And now that you've insulted my fiancé and myself, there's no way you're coming to the wedding."

"As you know, the double wedding is the biggest thing to happen in Hollywood society in years. There will be so many people there, one more probably won't be noticed."

"Do not even think about showing up at my wedding," Jean said.

"Invite me."

"It's not going to happen."

"I'll be there one way or another."

She stormed out of the restaurant and drove directly to Maggie's.

"What's going on?" Maggie asked when she opened the door.

"I just had lunch with Thomas O'Leary."

"You *what*?"

"I know, I know. He called me so I went."

"What did he want?" Maggie asked.

"He wants me to invite him to the wedding."

"Is he crazy? Why would we do that?"

"Exactly. I told him that. He said he'll show up whether we invite him or not."

"That's not right. How can we keep him out?"

"I don't know. I'll talk to David tomorrow night."

After filming Monday, Jean asked David if they could go to dinner. Over dinner, she brought up her conversation with Thomas O'Leary.

"He's got a lot of nerve," David said.

"I know. Is there any way we can keep him out?"

"I suppose we could hire security, but really, how do we know who's going to be there? We invited hundreds of people and they're all bringing guests. What would we tell security?"

"We could just give them a picture of O'Leary and tell them not to let him in."

"That might work. I'll hire a firm."

"Thanks. I knew you'd have a solution."

❖

The big day arrived. The guest list read like a Who's Who of Hollywood. There were legends from days gone by as well as up-and-coming stars of the day. And of course, all the current day headliners were there.

Jean's father walked her down the aisle, while Maggie had Mr. Goldsmith do the honors for her. Jean had a difficult time keeping her focus in front of her rather than casting sidelong glances at the radiant Maggie. She was a sight to behold, and Jean wished it was Maggie she got to kiss when the ceremony ended.

She kept it together and kept her gaze firmly planted on David who looked smashing in his black tux. She knew he was lusting after Spencer who was as handsome a man as Jean had ever seen. They would make a gorgeous couple, as would she and Maggie. It was just a matter of getting through the wedding and then the games could begin.

It was on shaky legs that Jean stood holding David's hands. The ceremony was beautiful, with an excellent preacher, but still, Jean just wanted it over. She wanted to be married to a man so she could have more freedom to live her life unquestioned. When it was time to repeat the vows, Jean looked into David's eyes, but thought only of Maggie. She was pledging her life to her, just as surely as David was pledging his life to Spencer. The ceremony was finally over, they walked down the aisle, hand in hand along with Spencer and Maggie. The crowd cheered loudly, clearly excited at the new beginning this meant for them. Little did they know. Little did Jean care.

It was time for the first dance, and they all made their way to the dance floor. They all put on the performances of their lives as they danced, looking like they were head over heels in love with their new spouses. The cameras flashed and almost blinded Jean, but she danced on. She couldn't wait for the party to end so she could have some quiet time with Maggie. She cautioned herself to stay in the present, that time with Maggie would be there soon enough.

They cut their cakes with great production. Jean's hip brushed against Maggie's as they bent to make that first cut. The sparks flew. She forced herself not to look at her right then, as she knew that look would be captured in a dozen pictures and there could be no denying it. So, she simply fed David a piece of cake and accepted her piece before waltzing around the dance floor again.

Jean lost count of how many dance partners she'd had. Her legs and feet were sore after several hours, yet she kept on dancing. The atmosphere was festive, so much so that she didn't notice David talking to one of the security guards. He cut in on her dance.

"O'Leary tried to get in. They turned him away," he said.

"Do you think he'll leave?"

"I don't know. If he wants to be here, I'd anticipate him trying a different tactic. I just can't get over the nerve of him trying to crash our wedding."

"No kidding. We have a lot of very important, very famous people here. These people don't need to be compromised or made to feel uncomfortable," Jean said.

"He needs to give up his witch-hunt. I, for one, am tired of it. And now we're legit in the eyes of the law and most of this city. He needs to forget about us."

"Yes, but he's not stupid, David."

"That's what makes him so dangerous."

The song ended and David danced with Maggie while Spencer took Jean for a spin.

"What were you two talking about?" Spencer asked. "You looked so serious."

"O'Leary tried to get in."

"Here?"

"Yes, here. Security kept him out, but still…"

"I'm sure he won't get in. This is a big day for the four of us, Jean. We should just relax and revel in it."

That dance finally ended and Jean wandered over to the champagne fountain.

"Fancy meeting you here," Maggie said.

"Oh, Maggie. It's so good to be able to talk to you. Are you having fun?"

"I am. I'm dancing like a fool and talking to so many famous people, my head is spinning." She lowered her voice. "Though I'm looking forward to all this being over so we can go to Palm Springs for our honeymoon."

"I know what you mean. I suppose we should be leaving soon. The guests will be getting antsy to leave and we have to leave first."

"I'm ready when you are."

"Let's check with the guys."

CHAPTER TWELVE

After Jean and Maggie changed into traveling clothes, David and Spencer escorted them to the rented Rolls Royce. Their bags were already loaded in the trunk so they set off for Palm Springs. The mood was high in the car, with all four excited about the beginning of their new lives together. The ranch just outside of Hollywood was completed so they'd all live together after their honeymoon. Everything was in place for them.

They arrived in Palm Springs to many photographers waiting outside the hotel. They paused for more pictures and signed a few autographs before checking in. The hotel had one honeymoon suite, so they got two regular suites with an adjoining door.

Once they were settled in as the public expected, Jean took a few items into the room she'd share with Maggie. She stared at Maggie, dressed in a green skirt suit. She found herself getting lost in her eyes.

"Doll, you look amazing," she said.

"So do you. I can't believe this is really happening. All our plans are working out. Our dreams are coming true."

"Yes, they are. We've earned this happiness."

"That we have."

Jean took Maggie into a soft embrace and held her. She smelled the familiar scent of lavender and vanilla that wafted from her hair. She tilted Maggie's chin up slightly, forcing their gazes to meet. She lowered her mouth and lightly brushed her lips with her own. The feeling of their mouths meeting caused gooseflesh on her skin.

"I need you, darling," Maggie said.

"I need you."

Jean unbuttoned Maggie's jacket and hung it in the closet. She made short order of the buttons on Maggie's blouse and laid it over the back of a chair.

Maggie stood in her bra and skirt and Jean didn't know what to do next. Did she want to take off her bra and have at her supple breasts? Or did she want to get rid of her skirt and delve into the heaven she knew was underneath.

She opted to slip her bra off and sucked a hard nipple.

"Oh, darling. You make me feel so good," Maggie said.

"I've dreamed of doing this all day. Ever since I saw you in your gown this morning."

"You looked beautiful in yours, too, Jean."

"Thanks, doll." Jean kissed her again and played over her breasts with her fingers. They responded by hardening more, and Jean played with the bumps that covered them. She lowered her head and took Maggie's nipple in her mouth again. She sucked it hard. She needed more and sucked harder and harder. She flicked her tongue over the tip of the nipple and felt Maggie's hands in her hair.

She eased Maggie onto the bed and ran her hand under her skirt.

"Oh, doll. You're so ready for me," Jean said.

"Always, my darling."

Jean withdrew her hand and unzipped Maggie's skirt. She wanted to see her naked, needed to see her whole body laid bare for her.

Once Maggie lay exposed, Jean stood and stripped off her own traveling suit and fell on top of her. The heat of their skin contact almost burned in its intensity.

"Dear God, I love you." Jean kissed down Maggie's cheeks, her chin, her neck, and chest. "I can't get enough of you. I need more. I crave more. Oh, God, Maggie."

Maggie was writhing under Jean, arching into her as she kissed her, pressing herself against her for more contact. Jean melted into Maggie. She needed to feel every inch of her. She rolled over and pulled Maggie on top of her. She brought her knee up and pressed it into Maggie. She was warm and wet and the feel of her spurned Jean on. She ran her hands up and down Maggie's sides. They were so soft and smooth. She loved the feel of Maggie's skin.

Jean pulled Maggie down and sucked on her nipples. First one and then the other, she pulled them deep into her mouth. She felt Maggie grow wetter and she was equally as drenched. She knew they'd both need release soon, but it was their wedding night and she wanted to make it last as long as she could.

"You're my wife now, Maggie," Jean said. "I married you today, not David."

"I know, darling. I'm married to you. And I love it."

"And I want our wedding night to be special, oh so special."

"Take me, Jean. Show me how much you love me."

"I'm going to."

She flipped Maggie over onto her stomach and climbed on top of her again. She pressed her breasts into Maggie's back as she kissed the nape of her neck. She pulled Maggie up and pressed her flesh into her ass. She reached her hand between her legs and entered her. She went deep inside her, further than ever before.

"Oh, my God, you're filling me. That feels amazing."

"Oh, doll, you feel so good. Take me. Take all of me."

Jean inserted another finger, using four to please Maggie. She bit Maggie's back, frantic in her desire. She sucked and licked up and down her back as she continued to thrust in and out of her. She thought she'd collapse from her own arousal. She was close to release, but wanted to make sure to bring Maggie to her climax first.

Jean felt Maggie clench hard, grasping around her fingers as her first orgasm hit. Jean continued to plunge inside her as Maggie came over and over. Jean flipped Maggie over and climbed between her legs. She licked her clean before focusing on her still swollen clit. She lapped at it a few times before Maggie cried out again.

Maggie lay quietly with no sound but her heavy breathing. Jean was beside herself with need by that time, but she let Maggie pull herself together. When Maggie finally reached for her, she spread her legs wide. Maggie was in her and on her and around her. Jean couldn't tell where her fingers were. She only knew she never wanted the pleasure to end. She clung to the sheets as the waves of her climax washed over her.

They slept for an hour and then took a shower together to get ready for dinner. In the shower, Jean took her time lathering up her hands. She massaged Maggie from top to bottom, paying special attention to between her legs. Maggie held on to Jean as the new round of orgasms hit. They rinsed off and joined the men in their room for drinks.

"How was your evening?" David asked.

"It was nice. We had a much needed nap," Jean said.

"Good. Are you ready to make our appearance for dinner?" Spencer said.

"We are," Maggie said.

"Excellent. You both look very nice, by the way," David said.

They finished their champagne and took the elevator to the main floor. The press presence at the dining room was almost overwhelming. Jean held tightly to David's hand, as she felt Maggie pressed into her back. Having Maggie there made it all bearable.

Each couple took a turn smiling for the cameras before making their way to their seats. The restaurant was fairly empty at that hour so there were very few people asking for their autographs. Dinner was quiet and delicious.

"So what do you think ever happened with O'Leary today?" Jean asked.

"Did he show up?" Maggie said.

"He did, but security got rid of him."

"I don't know if we've heard the last from him," David said.

"Can't we do something to make him leave us alone?" Maggie said.

"Not while he's on this witch-hunt. He's investigating what he thinks is a legitimate cause. We can do nothing but be careful and hope he forgets about us."

"I can see wanting to get rid of commies, but what's wrong with people like us?" Maggie asked.

"Nothing," David said. "Unfortunately, others don't feel that way."

"Well, I don't understand it," Maggie said.

"We just have to remain vigilant. Though our house is far enough removed from the city there shouldn't be too many curious people getting too close to us."

"That was sure genius of you to build a ranch out there," Maggie said. "I can't wait to make it a home."

After dinner, they went back to their rooms.

❖

Jean was as hungry for Maggie as her first time, but she took her time, loving her sweetly and completely. She worshiped her body, kissing every inch of her. When she could take no more, she lightly dragged her fingers over the length of her. She plunged them deep inside. She stroked her with a fervor that showed her own desire.

Maggie soon cried Jean's name as she came. Jean held her close and they fell into a fitful sleep.

The next day, they went horseback riding and soaked in the hot springs. They had the springs to themselves, which got Jean's libido roaring. She pulled Maggie close and kissed her hard on the mouth.

"I need you now," she said.

"Jean, this is a public place. It's not safe."

"No one's near here. We have the whole place to ourselves."

"But someone could walk in any minute."

"I'll be careful."

Jean was not to be deterred. She kissed Maggie again as her fingers found the crotch of her swimsuit. She deftly pulled it to the side and teased Maggie's opening. She felt her creaminess and knew she wanted it as badly as she did.

"You say no, but your body says yes."

"You know you get me excited," Maggie said.

"I love it." She slipped her fingers inside, then slowly withdrew them and played them across her clit.

"Oh, God, Jean. I can't hold out."

"Don't. Let it go, doll."

"But I'm scared."

"There's no one here. Let it go. Come for me."

Maggie threw her head back and held tightly to Jean as the climax hit. Jean got Maggie's suit back in place just as two other women entered the springs.

"Timing," Jean whispered.

Maggie blushed.

They soaked for a few more minutes and got out, feeling calm and relaxed. They met the men at the pool.

"How were the hot springs?" Spencer asked.

Maggie blushed again.

"That good, huh?" David laughed.

"They were very relaxing," Jean said.

"Well, come on in the pool. It feels great," David said.

They stripped out of their robes and climbed into the pool. The water was chilly, causing Maggie's nipples to harden.

"I love it when you're cold like this," Jean whispered in her ear.

Maggie blushed one more time.

"You're horrible," she said.

"You thought I was wonderful back at the springs."

"You were wonderful. You're wonderfully horrible. How's that?"

"I can accept that. I can't wait to get you back to the room."

"I can't wait, either."

They swam up to the bar and each had a glass of champagne. They toasted each other.

"Here's to us," Jean said.

"Yes," Maggie said. "To us."

They swam for an hour, until it was time to get ready for dinner.

Jean and Maggie went into their room to shower. Jean pulled Maggie on the bed with her.

"Come here. Let's have some fun."

"We have to get ready for dinner," Maggie argued.

"We have time. We always have time."

Jean stripped Maggie's suit off her and moved her hand all over her exposed body. She was still chilled from the pool, but eventually warmed at Jean's touches. Soon she was moving around under her, arching to get more contact.

Maggie spread her legs and begged Jean to be touched. Jean was more than happy to oblige. She slid her hand along Maggie's hard clit and pressed into it. Maggie moved in time with Jean and soon cried out in pleasure.

"We really do need to take showers now," Jean said.

They met the men downstairs at the bar. The place was fairly busy, but not so much that they couldn't find David and Spencer. The four of them stood in the middle of the bar visiting.

"Good evening. Aren't the four of you dashing?"

They turned to see Thomas O'Leary standing there.

"I think we are." David put his arm around Jean. "We're the happiest couples you'll ever meet."

"I see. Only which ones of you are actually the couples?"

"We are just as you see us, O'Leary."

"I don't believe you. I'll never believe you. It's my mission to prove what a farce you are."

"Mr. O'Leary," Jean said. "Please. We're on our honeymoon. Please leave us alone to enjoy it."

"I'm not going to leave you alone. I'll never leave you alone until my mission is complete."

"I agree with Jean," David said. "Let us enjoy our honeymoon."

"Well, if it's your honeymoon, why not let me see your suites? Is it true that you have adjoining suites?"

"It is true," David said. "And they're our private rooms. We don't need anyone seeing them."

"I just think if you'd let me prove to the world that these are legitimate marriages, you'd be able to go about your business from now on."

"No one questions our marriages but you. And you need to leave us alone. Please don't make us call the police on you for harassment."

"You haven't heard the last of me," O'Leary said as he walked off.

The mood was tense, but lightened by the time they were shown to their table for dinner. Several fans asked for autographs, and other stars stopped by to offer congratulations.

Jean went through the motions, but all she could think about was getting Maggie back to their room. Maggie looked stunning in a low-cut dress that made Jean want to lick the exposed skin. She tried to focus on the conversation, but it was simply more like a steady buzz in the back of her mind. In the forefront was her desire for Maggie.

Dinner finally ended and the men escorted them out of the restaurant and up to their rooms.

"Good night, you two." Jean took Maggie's hand and led her through the door to their room.

"I couldn't keep my eyes off you all night," Jean said. "I hope no one got a picture of that, because they'd surely see the hunger in my eyes."

"Oh, Jean. You say the sweetest things."

"I mean it. I wanted to devour you before we even left the room. Every moment downstairs was sheer torment."

"Well, we're not downstairs anymore."

"No, we're not." Jean closed the distance between them. "We're all alone, away from prying eyes."

"I like that."

"So do I."

She ran her hands up and down Maggie's bare arms, amazed as always, at how soft and smooth they were. She clasped her hands and lowered her mouth, claiming Maggie's. She ran her tongue across Maggie's lips, prying them open and gaining access to the warm moist area inside.

The world tilted slightly when their tongues met and Jean fought to stay upright. Every kiss was like the first with Maggie, each touch unique. She couldn't breathe in her excitement. All she could do was focus on the joining with Maggie. For now it was just a kiss, but soon, it would be a joining of bodies and souls as they took each other higher than ever before.

She walked Maggie back to the bed and bent to kiss the exposed skin she'd longed for all night. Her skin was soft as cotton and smooth as silk. She kissed and nibbled on it until she could take no more.

Jean unzipped Maggie's dress and carefully laid it over a chair. She walked back to Maggie and let Maggie unzip her dress. She let it fall to the floor and stepped out of it. They stood there in their undergarments and Jean was breathless as she stared at Maggie's figure so beautifully on display.

"I'll never get enough of you," Jean said.

"I hope not," Maggie said. "I hope you'll always want more."

"I will, doll. I will always want more of you."

She kissed Maggie again and reached around to unhook her bra. Maggie's breasts heaved out of it, and Jean brought her hands around to support them. She ran her thumbs over her hardening nipples, aroused by their response to her touch. She cupped the full mounds in her hands and bent to taste one nipple and then the other.

"You're overdressed, darling," Maggie said.

She unhooked Jean's bra while Jean continued to suckle her. She reached under Jean to play with her breasts while Jean focused her attention on her own.

"Doll, no," Jean said. "I can't concentrate."

"Sorry, but I get to play, too. And your breasts are so big and beautiful. I can't contain myself."

"Let's just get the rest of our clothes off and climb into bed," Jean said.

"Sounds good to me."

They stripped out of what little they were wearing and lay on the bed. They were on their sides, facing each other. Jean reached out a hand and placed it behind Maggie's head. She drew her toward her, softly yet deliberately.

Their mouths met and their tongues danced in a tango filled with passion. Jean pulled herself up and rolled on top of Maggie, never breaking the kiss. She moved her hips against Maggie in time with her tongue moving inside her mouth.

She rolled over and pulled Maggie on top of her. She ran her hands up and down Maggie's back, feeling her soft curves, down to her shapely ass. She kneaded the soft flesh she found there as she felt herself growing wetter.

Jean bent a knee and Maggie slid along her thigh. Up and down she moved, pressing herself into Jean.

"Oh, yeah, doll. That's right. Oh, God, you're so damned sexy."

Maggie closed her eyes and continued her rubbing. Jean reached up and played with her nipples while she moved. The sight of Maggie was about to be Jean's undoing.

"Doll, here, slide off me."

"No. Too close."

Jean slipped her fingers between her leg and Maggie and pressed them into Maggie's engorged clit.

"Oh, darling. Oh, my God darling. That's it. Oh, yes. Oh, God yes." Maggie threw her head back and closed her eyes and Jean smiled in contentment. It was always an honor to make Maggie come. Every single time, she felt awed and humbled at being the one Maggie chose to take her to those mind shattering orgasms.

Maggie climbed off Jean.

"That was amazing."

"I'm so glad," Jean said. "You are so beautiful in those moments just before you come."

Maggie blushed.

"I don't know about that. I'm usually close to losing consciousness. I can't imagine that being pretty."

"It is. You're gorgeous."

"And now it's your turn to show me what you look like right before you climax."

"Haven't you seen that enough by now?" Jean said.

"Never enough, my love. Never enough."

Jean kissed Maggie hard on the mouth and then surrendered, allowing her to explore her body. Maggie moved her mouth down the length of Jean, finally settling between her legs. Jean's whole body was filled with current, the anticipation of what was to come was electrical.

Maggie licked Jean from end to end as she lapped at her clit and dipped her tongue inside.

"You taste amazing," she said.

"Oh, please. Don't stop."

Maggie grinned and looked at Jean.

"Are you saying I can't talk to you?"

"Oh, please, Doll. Not now. Please, no talking."

"But maybe I'm in the mood to chat with you."

Jean lay back on the pillow. She was breathing heavily.

"Dear God, no. Please, Maggie."

"If you insist."

Maggie went back to work on Jean and soon Jean was clutching the sheets and screaming Maggie's name. Maggie climbed up next to her on the bed.

"What the hell was that about?" Jean said. "Starting a conversation when I was teetering on the edge?"

"I don't know what came over me. I just felt like teasing you."

"That was just cruel," Jean said.

Maggie laughed.

"Poor baby. I still got you there, didn't I?"

"Yes, you did." Jean pulled Maggie close. "Yes, you did."

The honeymoon went on for a week, with tennis, horseback riding, hot springs, and pool time. They made a point to make appearances as couples, but for the most part Jean spent her time with Maggie and let David and Spencer have their time.

Chapter Thirteen

The honeymoon finally ended and they moved into a five thousand square foot ranch house just outside of the city limits. The main portion of the home was furnished with a massive living room, den, and dining room. The kitchen had all the modern day accoutrements, though none of them were much in the way of cooks. They hired on someone from a recommendation of a friend of David's. It was someone who was good at cooking and cleaning and yet also discreet, which was paramount for the four of them.

The house sat on an acre, most of which was prime for gardening. Jean couldn't wait to start planting to make the outside of their home the paradise the inside would be. There was also an Olympic-sized swimming pool under some palms on the west side of the house which they used all the time. There was an outdoor bar, too, so cocktails were often combined with swimming after a hard day at work. And the four of them always had dinner together in their dining room.

The rest of the inside of the house was private quarters. David and Spencer shared one wing and Jean and Maggie shared another. Each wing had three bedrooms and a study. Jean and Maggie filled their study with bookshelves and bought all the current books. They also bought older books by the likes of Edna St. Vincent Millay.

Jean and Maggie enjoyed their private quarters every night. The first night they were there, they broke in the new house the way only the two of them could. They started in the library on the settee. Jean snuck up behind Maggie while she was looking at some of the books on the shelf. She grabbed her buttocks and squeezed while she kissed her neck.

"Mm. I love you, doll."

"I love you, too. I love this room. I didn't realize you had so many books."

"I love to read."

"I know this. I just didn't realize how much, I guess."

Jean spun Maggie around and kissed her on her mouth, pressing her against her.

"I need you," she said.

"Then take me."

Jean unzipped Maggie's skirt and took her blouse over her head. Maggie returned the favor, slipping Jean's slacks to the floor and unbuttoning her shirt.

"I love how you dress in private," Maggie said.

"I need to be comfortable."

"I need to get comfortable with you right now."

Jean pulled her on to the settee and resumed kissing her. She moved her hands all around her body, up and down and around and around. She didn't stop until Maggie was begging for more.

Finally, she slid her hand between Maggie's legs. She entered her deep and fast, enjoying the feeling of Maggie wrapped around her. She pressed her thumb into Maggie's clit and Maggie cried out as she closed around Jean again and again.

They continued their play through the two spare bedrooms until they finally arrived in their master. This time it was Maggie who took charge and climbed on top of Jean. She kissed her mouth and neck, then moved down her chest to a pert nipple. She drew it deep in her mouth and ran her tongue over the tip. She flicked it several times before she kissed lower. She climbed between Jean's legs and stared at her.

"My God, you're beautiful," she said.

"Don't tease me, Maggie."

Maggie put Jean's legs over her shoulders and bent to taste her. She sucked Maggie's lower lips and ran her tongue between them. She buried her tongue deep inside and licked every inch. She moved to Jean's clit and took it between her lips. She licked it hard and fast until Jean screamed.

They fell into a fitful sleep in their new home, happy, safe, and sound.

❖

The four of them lived together very well. They threw lavish parties where Hollywood's premier celebrities would rub elbows with up and coming stars. Their house was known as the party headquarters. However, both wings were locked off at all times during the parties. No one ever questioned it. It was simply how it was.

Thomas O'Leary finally gave up on them and started barking up another Hollywood tree. They felt bad for his new targets but were happy to have him out of their lives.

Maggie had begun to headline movies, which made all of them proud. Jean continued to be America's Sweetheart, unscathed. And the celebration when Jean won an Academy Award surpassed even their wedding reception.

Life was good for all of them for many years. On June 28, 1994, sadness closed on the house. After living together for almost fifty years, Spencer passed away from pneumonia. Jean, Maggie, and David were crushed. Jean tried to be strong for David and Maggie, but it wasn't easy. David was lost. He was a shell blowing in the wind. He passed the following Christmas Eve. The doctors said otherwise, but Jean knew he'd died from a broken heart.

No one thought twice about Jean and Maggie keeping the house by themselves. Times were different. There were no Thomas O'Learys in the world. There were now paparazzi planted all over town and they took pictures of the two whenever they went out. In the blurbs about the pictures, they were mentioned as Hollywood royalty. No one made accusations or insinuations. Jean loved living in this new age.

They traveled often and often reflected on the days when they first met and how trips to Palm Springs were considered vacations. They traveled all over the world, via plane or ship. And even sharing quarters on a ship didn't raise eyebrows.

They took a two and a half week cruise around South America in 2001. Although they were older, the passion still burned. And the Latin American lifestyles they saw fanned the flame. They made love slowly and tenderly in their cabin, Jean still overwhelmed with desire for Maggie.

"I love you so much," she said. "I will never tire of loving you."

"Make love to me, Jean."

"Gladly."

Jean softly and carefully pleased Maggie. She took her again to the heights most people only dreamed of. Maggie settled into her arms after.

"Who'd have thought we'd still be making love after all these years?"

"I did. I never doubted for a moment that I'd want you forever."

"Oh, Jean. You say the sweetest things. You still make my heart melt."

"We're lucky we still have our health," Jean said. "That's important."

"True. If I had a bad hip, there's no way you could do what you just did."

Jean laughed and blushed.

"No, I suppose I couldn't."

The cruise was one of the highlights of their life together.

Time passed and they continued loving each other. They were seen in public more often, and occasionally the paparazzi would print something questioning their sexuality, but no one seemed to care. They followed the news and knew that gay rights were a big issue in the country and that so many more people were tolerant of gays and lesbians. It seemed like it was easier every year to be a lesbian.

One day in 2008, Maggie was napping and Jean was watching the news. The reporter came on with breaking news. Same sex marriage was legal in California. Jean left a note for Maggie that she was running errands and left the house.

She drove to her favorite jewelry store and picked out the most beautiful diamond ring she could find. It wasn't the biggest or gaudiest, but it was the most beautiful because it would look perfect on Maggie's small hands.

Jean arrived back at the house to find Maggie in the kitchen making tea.

"Hey, doll," Jean said.

"Hello. Where'd you take off to?"

Jean led Maggie into the living room and had her sit on the big black sofa.

"What are you up to, Jean Sanders?"

"I'm sorry I can't kneel," Jean said. "I'd never get up again."

"What is going on?"

Jean presented Maggie with the ring.

"Maggie Cranston, will you marry me?"

"You know I would if I could."

"You can. Same sex marriage is legal in California now. So say yes. Please say yes."

"Oh, my God, yes, Jean. Yes, yes, yes."

Jean slipped the ring on Maggie. It fit her perfectly. Jean knew it would. She knew Maggie's finger size just as she knew everything else about her. Maggie looked at the ring.

"Oh, Jean. It's beautiful."

"I thought it was you," Jean said.

"It really is. So when will we get married? Will we have a big wedding? What about our bands? We have things to think about."

"I was thinking about getting married at the courthouse. You know, have a justice of the peace perform it. And we can have some friends over to help us celebrate."

"That sounds perfect. But we need to pick out our bands."
Jean laughed.

"You're kind of stuck on the bands, aren't you? We can go right now and pick out our bands, if you'd like."

They went back to the jewelry store and picked out their bands. Maggie insisted they be engraved, so each one said, "A marriage sixty-two years in the making."

On June sixteenth, they were among the first at the courthouse to get their licenses. Jean held Maggie's hand tightly, determined to protect her if things got ugly. But she needn't have worried. Everything went smoothly and soon they were married. They were all smiles as they walked out into the morning air to the flashes of cameras. This time they could stop and smile, holding each other's hands for all to see. There was no fear, no sense of shame. There was just joy and love.

Some people were picketing across the street, but they paid no attention to them. Jean wrapped her arm around Maggie and held her close as they crossed the street to their car. They drove back to their house, where many of their friends had gathered to help them celebrate the happiest day of their lives.

There were young celebrities and older ones. Very few of their costars from their glory days were able to make it. A few could, but others were either gone or invalids. But the younger generation was well represented and they were all supportive. And the few of the older stars that did make it couldn't have been happier for them.

The party lasted well into the night. The pool was full of revelers and the bartenders they'd hired were busy all night long. Jean and Maggie finally said good night and turned in. They slept as a married couple for the first time in their life.

The next morning over coffee, Jean and Maggie were reading the paper. Jean set her paper down.

"Do you feel any different?" she asked.

"Not really. Maybe a little. I don't know."

"I don't, really. Somewhat. I think I just feel validated. That's the word. And happy. Happier than I've ever been to have you as my wife."

"And, God willing, we'll be wives for many years to come," Maggie said.

"Amen to that."

About the Author

MJ Williamz is the author of seven books including Goldie Award winners *Initiation by Desire* and *Escapades*. She has also had over thirty short stories published, mostly erotica, with a few romances and one or two horrors thrown in for good measure.

When not writing, MJ can be found relaxing with her wife and son in Houston, TX.

Check out her website at www.mjwilliamz.com, follow her on Twitter at @mj_williamz or friend her on Facebook.

Books Available from Bold Strokes Books

Illicit Artifacts by Stevie Mikayne. Her foster mother's death cracked open a secret world Jil never wanted to see…and now she has to pick up the stolen pieces. (978-1-62639-4-728)

Pathfinder by Gun Brooke. Heading for their new homeworld, Exodus's chief engineer Adina Vantressa and nurse Briar Lindemay carry game-changing secrets that may well cause them to lose everything when disaster strikes. (978-1-62639-4-445)

Prescription for Love by Radclyffe. Dr. Flannery Rivers finds herself attracted to the new ER chief, city girl Abigail Remy, and the incendiary mix of city and country, fire and ice, tradition and change is combustible. (978-1-62639-5-701)

Ready or Not by Melissa Brayden. Uptight Mallory Spencer finds relinquishing control to bartender Hope Sanders too tall an order in fast-paced New York City. (978-1-62639-4-438)

Summer Passion by MJ Williamz. Women loving women is forbidden in 1946 Hollywood, yet Jean and Maggie strive to keep their love alive and away from prying eyes. (978-1-62639-5-404)

The Princess and the Prix by Nell Stark. "Ugly duckling" Princess Alix of Monaco was resigned to loneliness until she met race car driver Thalia d'Angelis. (978-1-62639-4-742)

Winter's Harbor by Aurora Rey. Lia Brooks isn't looking for love in Provincetown, but when she discovers chocolate croissants and pastry chef Alex McKinnon, her winter retreat quickly starts heating up. (978-1-62639-4-988)

The Time Before Now by Missouri Vaun. Vivian flees a disastrous affair, embarking on an epic, transformative journey to escape her past, until destiny introduces her to Ida, who helps her rediscover trust, love, and hope. (978-1-62639-446-9)

Twisted Whispers by Sheri Lewis Wohl. Betrayal, lies, and secrets—whispers of a friend lost to darkness. Can a reluctant psychic set things right or will an evil soul destroy those she loves? (978-1-62639-439-1)

The Courage to Try by C.A. Popovich. Finding love is worth getting past the fear of trying. (978-1-62639-528-2)

Break Point by Yolanda Wallace. In a world readying for war, can love find a way? (978-1-62639-568-8)

Countdown by Julie Cannon. Can two strong-willed, powerful women overcome their differences to save the lives of seven others and begin a life they never imagined together? (978-1-62639-471-1)

Keep Hold by Michelle Grubb. Claire knew some things should be left alone and some rules should never be broken, but the most forbidden, well, they are the most tempting. (978-1-62639-502-2)

Deadly Medicine by Jaime Maddox. Dr. Ward Thrasher's life is in turmoil. Her partner Jess left her, and her job puts her in the path of a murderous physician who has Jess in his sights. (978-1-62639-424-7)

New Beginnings by KC Richardson. Can the connection and attraction between Jordan Roberts and Kirsten Murphy be enough for Jordan to trust Kirsten with her heart? (978-1-62639-450-6)

Officer Down by Erin Dutton. Can two women who've made careers out of being there for others in crisis find the strength to need each other? (978-1-62639-423-0)

Reasonable Doubt by Carsen Taite. Just when Sarah and Ellery think they've left dangerous careers behind, a new case sets them—and their hearts—on a collision course. (978-1-62639-442-1)

Tarnished Gold by Ann Aptaker. Cantor Gold must outsmart the Law, outrun New York's dockside gangsters, outplay a shady art dealer, his lover, and a beautiful curator, and stay out of a killer's gun sights. (978-1-62639-426-1)

The Renegade by Amy Dunne. Post-apocalyptic survivors Alex and Evelyn secretly find love while held captive by a deranged cult, but when their relationship is discovered, they must fight for their freedom—or die trying. (978-1-62639-427-8)

Thrall by Barbara Ann Wright. Four women in a warrior society must work together to lift an insidious curse while caught between their own desires, the will of their peoples, and an ancient evil. (978-1-62639-437-7)

White Horse in Winter by Franci McMahon. Love between two women collides with the inner poison of a closeted horse trainer in the green hills of Vermont. (978-1-62639-429-2)

Autumn Spring by Shelley Thrasher. Can Bree and Linda, two women in the autumn of their lives, put their hearts first and find the love they've never dared seize? (978-1-62639-365-3)

The Chameleon's Tale by Andrea Bramhall. Two old friends must work through a web of lies and deceit to find themselves again, but in the search they discover far more than they ever went looking for. (978-1-62639-363-9)

Side Effects by VK Powell. Detective Jordan Bishop and Dr. Neela Sahjani must decide if it's easier to trust someone with your heart or your life as they face threatening protestors, corrupt politicians, and their increasing attraction. (978-1-62639-364-6)

Warm November by Kathleen Knowles. What do you do if the one woman you want is the only one you can't have? (978-1-62639-366-0)

In Every Cloud by Tina Michele. When Bree finally leaves her shattered life behind, is she strong enough to salvage the remaining pieces of her heart and find the place where it truly fits? (978-1-62639-413-1)

Rise of the Gorgon by Tanai Walker. When independent Internet journalist Elle Pharell goes to Kuwait to investigate a veteran's mysterious suicide, she hires Cassandra Hunt, an interpreter with a covert agenda. (978-1-62639-367-7)

Crossed by Meredith Doench. Agent Luce Hansen returns home to catch a killer and risks everything to revisit the unsolved murder of her first girlfriend and confront the demons of her youth. (978-1-62639-361-5)

Making a Comeback by Julie Blair. Music and love take center stage when jazz pianist Liz Randall tries to make a comeback with the help of her reclusive, blind neighbor, Jac Winters. (978-1-62639-357-8)

Soul Unique by Gun Brooke. Self-proclaimed cynic Greer Landon falls for Hayden Rowe's paintings and the young woman shortly after, but will Hayden, who lives with Asperger syndrome, trust her and reciprocate her feelings? (978-1-62639-358-5)

The Price of Honor by Radclyffe. Honor and duty are not always black and white—and when self-styled patriots take up arms against the government, the price of honor may be a life. (978-1-62639-359-2)

Mounting Evidence by Karis Walsh. Lieutenant Abigail Hargrove and her mounted police unit need to solve a murder and protect wetland biologist Kira Lovell during the Washington State Fair. (978-1-62639-343-1)

Threads of the Heart by Jeannie Levig. Maggie and Addison Rae-McInnis share a love and a life, but are the threads that bind them together strong enough to withstand Addison's restlessness and the seductive Victoria Fontaine? (978-1-62639-410-0)

Sheltered Love by MJ Williamz. Boone Fairway and Grey Dawson—two women touched by abuse—overcome their pasts to find happiness in each other. (978-1-62639-362-2)

Death's Doorway by Crin Claxton. Helping the dead can be deadly: Tony may be listening to the dead, but she needs to learn to listen to the living. (978-1-62639-354-7)

Searching for Celia by Elizabeth Ridley. As American spy novelist Dayle Salvesen investigates the mysterious disappearance of her ex-lover, Celia, in London, she begins questioning how well she knew Celia—and how well she knows herself. (978-1-62639-356-1).

Hardwired by C.P. Rowlands. Award-winning teacher Clary Stone and Leefe Ellis, manager of the homeless shelter for small children, stand together in a part of Clary's hometown that she never knew existed. (978-1-62639-351-6)

The Muse by Meghan O'Brien. Erotica author Kate McMannis struggles with writer's block until a gorgeous muse entices her into a world of fantasy sex and inadvertent romance. (978-1-62639-223-6)

No Good Reason by Cari Hunter. A violent kidnapping in a Peak District village pushes Detective Sanne Jensen and lifelong friend Dr. Meg Fielding closer, just as it threatens to tear everything apart. (978-1-62639-352-3)

The 45th Parallel by Lisa Girolami. Burying her mother isn't the worst thing that can happen to Val Montague when she returns to the woodsy but peculiar town of Hemlock, Oregon. (978-1-62639-342-4)

Romance by the Book by Jo Victor. If Cam didn't keep disrupting her life, maybe Alex could uncover the secret of a century-old love story, and solve the greatest mystery of all—her own heart. (978-1-62639-353-0)

A Royal Romance by Jenny Frame. In a country where class still divides, can love topple the last social taboo and allow Queen Georgina and Beatrice Elliot, a working-class girl, their happy ever after? (978-1-62639-360-8)

Bouncing by Jaime Maddox. Basketball coach Alex Dalton has been bouncing from woman to woman because no one ever held her interest, until she meets her new assistant, Britain Dodge. (978-1-62639-344-8)

All Things Rise by Missouri Vaun. Cole rescues a striking pilot who crash-lands near her family's farm, setting in motion a chain of events that will forever alter the course of her life. (978-1-62639-346-2)